THE STALKER
AND THE STALKED

Elossa looked down at the plaque of metal. Its surface was clear, but strangely enough did not reflect her face. There was a ripple on the mirror-not-mirror. There appeared on it the image of the fallen block of stone with the malignant face.

Reception was working. Now for her follower. Warily, very slowly, she sent out the questing thought.

It touched, held. There was a small figure on the surface of the disc. He was dressed in the leather of a Raski—a hunter, for he had a bow and a bow-case, though he also wore a short sword. His face she could not see, but the emanations of the mind-touch suggested he was young. And . . . **dangerous. DANGEROUS. . . .**

Yurth Burden

Andre Norton

Illustrated by Jack Gaughan

DAW BOOKS, INC.

DONALD A. WOLLHEIM, PUBLISHER

1633 Broadway, New York, NY 10019

DAW Book Collectors' Number 304

First DAW Printing, September 1978

5   6   7   8   9

1

The Raski girl made Demon Horns with two fingers
of her left hand and spat between them. That droplet
of moisture landed, dust covered, on the rutted clay
of the road just missing the edge of Elossa's stained
travel cloak. She did not look at the girl but kept her
eyes turned to those distant mountain rises, her goal.

In the town hate was a foul cloud to stifle her. She
should have avoided the village. None of Yurth blood
ever went into one of the native holdings if they
could help it. Broadcast hate so deep gnawed at one's
Upper Sense, clouded reception, muddied the thoughts.
But she had had to have food. A tumble on a stream's
stepping stones in the past evening dusk had turned
the supplies she carried in her belt pouch into a sticky
mess she had jettisoned that morning.

The merchant whose stall she had visited had been
surly and sullen. However, he had not had the courage to refuse her when she made a quick choice. All

those eyes, and the waves of hate. . . . Now, when she judged she was well beyond the girl who had given her that last salute, Elossa walked faster.

A Yurth man or woman moved with dignity among the Raski, just as they ignored the natives, looking over and around them as if they were not. Yurth and Raski were as different as light and dark, mountain and plain, heat and cold. There was no common ground for their meeting ever.

Yet they shared the same world, ate the same food, breathed the same air. Even some among her kin had dark hair resembling that the Raski wore in tight rolls about their heads, and their skins were not unlike in color. That of the Raski might be brown by birth, but the Yurth, living as they did ever under the sky and the fierce sun, also tanned darkly. Put a Yurth, even herself, into the bodice and ankle-sweeping skirt of the girl who had so graphically made her hate clear, let her hair grow and twist it up, and she might have looked no, or little, different. It was only in the mind, the thought, that Yurth stood apart.

It had always been so. The Upper Sense was a Yurth child's from birth. He or she was trained in its use before plain talk came from the lips. For the Upper Sense was all which stood between them and utter annihilation.

Zacar was not an easy world. Storms of terrible force came in the bleak season, sealing Yurth clans into their mountain burrows, blasting, and overwhelming the towns and the dwellings on the plains. Wind, hail, freezing winds, rain in drowning torrents. . . . All life sought shelter when those struck. That is why the Pilgrimage was only possible during the two months of early autumn, why she must hurry to find her goal.

Elossa dug her staff point into the crumbling clay and turned aside from the road which served farms she could see, the houses squatting drably some distance ahead. For the road, such as it was, angled away from the mountains she must reach. She longed to be out of the plains, higher up into the places of her own heritage, where one could breathe air untainted by dust, think thoughts unassailed by the hate which clogged about any Raski gathering place.

That she must make this journey alone was in keeping with the custom of her people. On the day the clan women had gathered to bring her staff, cloak, supply bag, she had known a sinking of heart which was not quite fear. To travel out into the unknown alone. . . . But that was the heritage of Yurth, and each girl and boy did so when their bodies were ready for the duties of Elders, their minds fallow enough to receive the Knowledge. Some never returned. Those who did were—changed.

They were able to set up barriers between themselves and their fellows, sealing out thought talk when they wished. Also they were graver, preoccupied, as if some part of the Knowledge, or perhaps the whole of it, had been a burden fastened on them. But they were Yurth, and as Yurth must return to the cradle of the clan, accept the Knowledge, however bitter or troublesome that might be.

It was the Knowledge which would itself guide them to their goal. They must leave their minds open until a thought thread would draw them. The coming of that was the command they must obey. She had tramped for four days now, the strange urgency working ever in her, bringing her by the shortest route across the plains to the mountains she now faced, the land no one visited now unless the Call came.

She had often speculated with those of her own birth age as to what must lie there. Two of their company had gone and returned. However, to ask them what they had done, or seen, was forbidden by custom. The barrier was already set in them. Thus the mystery always remained a mystery until one was led oneself to discover the truth.

Why did the Raski hate them so, Elossa wondered. It must be because of the Upper Sense. The plains dwellers lacked that. But there was something else. She was different from the hoose, the kannen, all the other life which Yurth respected and strove to aid. She did not wear upon her body, slender beneath her enveloping cloak, dust plastered from the road, fur or scales. Yet there was no hate for her in the minds of those others. Wariness, yes, if the creature was new come into the places of the clan. But that was natural. Why, then, did those who possessed bodies like her own beat at her with black hate in their bodies like her own beat at her with black hate in their thoughts if she was forced by some chance to move among them as she had done this morning?

Yurth did not seek to command—even those of lesser and weaker minds. All creatures had their limitations—even as did the Yurth. Some of her kin were keener witted, faster to mind-speak, producing thoughts which were new, unusual enough to make one chew upon them in solitude. But Yurth did not have rulers or ruled. There were customs, such as the Pilgrimage, which all followed when the time was ripe. Still no one ordered that this be so. Rather did those obeying such customs recognize within themselves that this must be done without question.

Twice, she had heard, in the years before her birth, long ago by the reckoning of the clan, the King-Head of the Raski had sent armies to seek out and destroy the Yurth. Once those reached the mountains they had fallen into the net of illusions which the Elders could weave at will.

Men broke out of disciplined companies, wandered lost, until they were subtly set back on their path again. Into the mind of the King-Head himself was inserted a warning. So that when his brave soldiers came straggling back, foot worn, exhausted, he returned to his city stronghold, and did not plan a third mountain expedition. Thereafter the Yurth were let strictly alone and the mountain land was theirs.

But among the Raski there were rulers and ruled, and they were, as far as Elossa had been able to tell, the sorrier for that. Some men and women toiled all their lives that others might live free and turn their hands to no task. That this was a part of their otherness was true, and perhaps those who toiled had little liking for it. Did they hate their masters with some of the same black hatred that they turned toward the Yurth? Was that hate rooted in a bitter and abiding envy of the freedom and fellowship of the clans? But how could that be, what Raski knew how the clans lived? They lacked the mind-speak and could not so rove away from their bodies to survey what lay at a distance.

Elossa quickened pace again. To be away from this! She was fanciful. Surely no tongue of that black ill-wishing she had "seen" with the Upper Sense reached after her like the claws of a sargon. Fancies such as that were for children, not one old enough to be summoned for the Pilgrimage. The sooner, however, that she was in the foothills, the more at ease she would be.

Thus she walked steadily as the fields about gave way from ordered rows of grain to pasturage, well grazed by hoose teeth. Those patient animals themselves raised their heads as she passed. She gave them silent greeting, which seemed so much to astound them that here and there one shook its head or snorted. A younger one came trotting to parallel her way, watching her, Elossa felt, wistfully. In its mind she detected a dim memory of running free with no rein or lead cord to check that racing.

She paused to give it the blessing of food forage and pleasant days. Back to her came wonder and pleasure in return. Here was one ruled, and yet those who ruled it did not know what manner of life it really was. Elossa wished that she might open the gate of all these pastures, let loose those the fences kept in restraint, that they might have the freedom only one remembered so dimly.

Yet it was also laid straightly upon the Yurth that they must not attempt to change in any way the life of the Raski or their servants. To do so meant using the Yurth gifts and talents in the wrong manner. Only in some crisis, to defend their own lives, might the Yurth cast illusions before their attackers.

Now the pastures disappeared; she entered the foothills of the mountains. The way was rough, but to Elossa it was familiar. She threw off the last of the shadow which had troubled her since she had come through the town. Lifting her head, she allowed the hood of her cloak to slip back so that the wind might run fingers through her pale, fine hair, bring fresh breath to her lungs.

She found faint traces of paths. Perhaps the townspeople came hunting here or they fed their stock among these hills. Yet there was no sign that such trails had been recently used. Then, upon climbing the top of one ascent, she sighted something else, a monolith taller than she when it stood upright, as it must once have been. It was not native to this place, for the rock was not the dull gray of that which surfaced here and through the scanty soil, rather a red, like the black-red of blood which had congealed in the sun.

Elossa shivered, wondering why such a dark thought had crossed her mind when she sighted that toppled stone. She shrank from it, so with the discipline of her kind she made herself approach closer. As she drew near she saw the rock had been carved, though time and erosion had blunted and worn those markings. What was left was only the suggestion of a head. Yet the longer Elossa stared at it, the more that same stifling uneasiness which had ridden her in the town arose to hasten her breathing, make her want to run.

The face was Raski in general outline, still it held some other element which was alien, dreadfully alien— threatening in spite of the veil the wearing of time had set upon it. A warning? Set here long ago to turn back the wayfarer, promising such danger ahead that its marker had been able to give it that distinctly evil cast?

The workmanship was not finished, smoothly done. Rather the rugged crudeness of its fashioning added to the force of the impression it made upon the viewer. Yes, it must be most decidedly a warning!

Elossa, with an effort, turned her back upon the thing, surveyed what lay beyond. With eyes taught by all her mountain training to study and evaluate terrain she caught another remnant of the far past: there had once been a road from this point on.

Stones had been buried by landslips, pushed aside by stubborn growth of bush and small tree. But the very grading which had been done for the placement of those stones had altered the natural contours of the land enough for her to be sure.

A road of stone? Such were only found near the cities of the King-Head. Labor in making such was very hard and would not have been wasted to fashion the entrance into the mountains, in the normal course of events. Also this was very, very old. Elossa went to the nearest of the stones, its edge upthrust as it lay nearly buried in the grass. She knelt and laid her hand upon it, reaching with thought to read. . . .

Faint, too faint to make any clear impression for her. This had returned to the wilds very long ago. So far in the past that the land had accepted it back, laid its own seal upon it. She could sense the trail of a sand lizard, the paw touch of a bander; what lay behind those in time was nothing she could seize upon.

The pavement itself headed for the mountain she

must climb, and to use the faint traces of it would lighten her way a little, aid to save her strength for the more difficult task ahead. Deliberately she turned into the roadway. Once a way of importance, it must have been sealed, forgotten, and the fallen monolith set to forbid entrance. Who had done this and why? The curiosity of Yurth minds possessed her; as she went she kept looking for any hint of what had been the purpose of this road.

The farther she advanced along the vestige of highway the more Elossa marveled at the skill and labor which had gone into its making. It did not take the easiest way, twisting and turning, as did the game trails and footpaths of the mountains she knew, or the clay-surfaced roads of the plains, rather it cut through all obstacles, as if its stubborn makers would tame the land to serve them.

She came to a place where slides had, in a measure, covered what had been a cut into the side of the mountain itself, picking her way over the debris left by those slides with a stout aid of her staff. Still the road headed in her direction, and, because her curiosity was now aroused, she determined to see where it might lead. Though it could be that before its goal was reached she must turn aside to fulfill her own quest.

There were no more of such worn-off stones as that left below, but at intervals she did sight small ones, several still upright. On those there were traces of carving, but so worn that the markings were only shadows. None of these gave her the feeling of discomfort as had the one below. Perhaps they had been set another time and certainly for other purposes.

It was in the shadow of such a one that Elossa sat to eat at nooning. She need not even use the liquid in her water flask, for only a short distance away a rill from some higher mountain spring had made a runnel for itself. The murmur of running water was loud enough to be heard. She felt at peace, at one with what lay about her.

Then—that peace was shattered!

Her mind-seek lazily reaching out to engulf the freedom and quiet, brushed upon thought! One of the clans on the same Pilgrimage? There were other clans cross mountain with whom her own people had little contact save during wintering. No, in that short touch she had not caught the familiar recognition which would have signaled Yurth—even Yurth traveling with a closed mind.

If it was not Yurth, then it was Raski. For no animal registered so. A hunter? She dared not probe, of course. Though the Raski hatred was dampened by fear, who knew what might chance were a Raski, away from his own kind, to encounter a single Yurth? She remembered now those on the Pilgrimage who had never returned. There were many explanations—a fall among rocks, a sickness away from all help, yes, even perhaps death by intent from some menace they could not restrain by the Upper Sense. Prudence must be her guide now.

Elossa pulled tight the string of her food bag, picked up her staff, got to her feet, No more easy way by the road. She must put her mountain knowledge to the test. No Raski had the skill of the Yurth in the heights. If she was indeed the quarry now, she was sure she could out-distance her trailer.

The girl began to climb, not with any spurt of speed—who knew—this chase might be a long one and she must conserve her strength. Also she could not stretch the power too far, keeping in touch with the pursuer and still sense out any trouble ahead. That lightest of mind-probes could only be made at intervals, to be sure she *was* being trailed and not that the other was going about some business of his own on the lower reaches.

2

At a point well above the forgotten road Elossa paused to take a breath or two, allow her mind-search to range below. Yes, he was still on a course which brought him in her wake. She frowned a little. Though she had taken precautions against such a thing yet she had not really believed it would happen. No Raski ever hunted Yurth. This trailing was unheard of among her people since the great defeat of the King-Head Philoar two generations ago. Why?

She could stop him, she believed. Illusion, mind-touch—oh, yes, if she wanted to bring her own talent into use, she had weapons enough. But there remained what lay ahead of her. When one set out upon the Pilgrimage there was no hint given by those who had made it of what might be expected. However, there were some warnings and orders, the foremost of those being that she would need all her talent to face what lay ahead.

It was the nature of the Upper Sense in itself that it was not a steady thing, always remaining at the same force no matter how one used it. No, it waxed and waned, must be stored against some sudden demand. She dared not exhaust what she might need later merely to turn back a stranger who might come this way by chance and did not really trail her.

Night was not far off and nights in the mountains were chill. Best find a place to hole up for the dark, cold hours. With eyes used to such a task, Elossa surveyed what lay ahead. So far this upward slope had not been enough to tax her strength greatly, but she noted that there were sharper rises beyond. Those she would leave, if she could, for the morning.

She now stood on a ledge which, to her right, widened out. Some drifts of soil there gave rootage to small bushes and grass. Bearing in that direction she came out into a pocket-sized meadow. The same stream which had given her drink near the ancient road fed a spring pool here. Her sweep of mind-search touched birds, several of the small rock-living rodents, nothing more formidable.

Dropping her staff and bag on the edge of the pool, Elossa knelt to splash the water over her face, wash away the clogging dust of the plains. She drank from cupped hands, then took from the breast of her jerkin a disc of metal depending from a twisted chain. Holding this flat on her palm, she gave a last survey, with eye and mind, of her immediate surroundings, making sure she dared to slacken her guard for a short time.

Nothing near which need be watched with caution, though perhaps she was indulging in folly to try this.

Still, it was best she knew who or what did follow. If the climber was a hunter, well enough. But Raski acting out of tradition—that was something else again.

She looked down at the plaque of metal. Its surface was clear, but strangely enough did not reflect her face. The disk remained completely blank. Elossa drew upon her power of concentration. Try first to envision something she knew existed in order to prove what she might later see was not just fancy born from her own imagination without her being aware.

The pillar of warning. There was a ripple on the mirror-not-mirror she held. Tiny, a little fuzzy, since distance also influenced reception, the fallen block of stone with a malignant face, now in more shadow with the passing of day, appeared.

Well enough, reception was working. Now for her follower, which would be a far more difficult task since she had never seen him and must project from mind-touch alone. Warily, very slowly, she sent out the questing thought.

It touched, held. She waited for a long moment. If the trailer were conscious of the probe there would be instant response. She would then break that tenuous linkage at once. But he did not react to her delicate probing. So, she applied a stronger send, staring down into the mirror.

Far more fuzzy than the pillar, yes, because she dared not reinforce the linkage past the power she now exerted. But there was a small figure on the mirror. He was dressed in the leather of a Raski—a hunter surely, for he had a bow and a bow case, though he also wore a short sword. His face she could not see, but the emanations of the mind-touch suggested he was young. And. . . .

Elossa blinked, instantly broke the contact. No, the response had not been that of Yurth. Yet that other had come to know that he was under her inspection—not clearly. He had been alerted only into uneasiness.

She considered that with a small measure of unbelief. By all the standards of her own people such awareness among the Raski was impossible. If they had had any of the Upper Sense they could never have been deceived by illusions. Still she was also certain that what she had read in those few moments before she had severed linkage had been right. He knew! Knew enough to sense she was probing.

Which made him dangerous. She could, of course, induce an illusion. It would not last long, no one Yurth had the power to hold such; it required a uniting of energy of many to produce that. But, she sat back and stared into the beginnings of a sunset. There were several illusions useful, the materialization of a sargon for example. No man could hope to stand up to one of those furred killers who killed to drink blood, and which were known to den among the heights. So insane were they that even Yurth could not control them more than to turn them for a space from the path they followed. They could not be mind-spoke, for they had not real minds only a chaos of blind ferocity and a devouring need for blood.

An excellent choice and. . . .

Elossa tensed. Sargon? But there *was* a sargon! Not downslope where she had thought to place her illusion, but up mountain. And it was headed toward her! Water—of course—water was needful to all life. This pool beside which she now sat might be the only water for some distance. She had noted the prints in its clay verge of wild birds as well as the lesser paw marks of the monu and mak. Water would draw the sargon.

Nor had this one eaten lately. The consciousness, such as this beast had, was all raging hunger near overwhelming thirst. Hunger, she must play upon that!

No sargon could be turned aside by illusion, and she could not alter its path either. The beast's hunger was too great. Swiftly she loosed mind-search. There was a rog, one of the dangerous beasts who also laired among the mountains. Was it too far away? Elossa could not be sure. It depended upon how hungry the sargon was.

Now working with precision, she fed into that swirling pit of ferocious desire the impression of the rog . . . near. . . . Not only would that mean food and blood to the rabid hunter, but rage at the invasion of what it considered its own hunting ground. For two great carnivores could not occupy the same territory without a battle—not two of these breeds.

She was succeeding! Elossa knew a flash of elation which she quickly dampened. Overconfidence was the worst error any Yurth might pay for. But the beast on the slope well above her had caught her suggestion, was angling away from the pool meadow. Now the wind blowing down mountain brought a trace of rank scent.

Rog, that way, she continued to beam. Yes, the sargon was definitely changing course. She must monitor, though, continue to. . . .

All this was a drain on her power which she had not foreseen.

Elossa held fast. The rank stench grew stronger. That the sargon could pick up her own body scent she did not fear. Long ago the Yurth had discovered various herbal infusions for both the skin and the inner parts of their bodies which destroyed the normal odors such beasts could pick up.

The sargon was running now, the momentum of downslope adding to its normal high speed when on a trail. Already it had passed the meadow and was well below her own position. It was time to withdraw that prick of mind-goad. There was a rog, sooner or later that. . . .

Her head jerked. The now gathering dusk in the lower reaches of the mountain might confuse sight but nothing could conceal that scream of rage and hunger. The rog so close . . . she had not thought it to be. . . .

Swiftly she strengthened her mind-probe and then froze.

Not the rog! Something to hunt, yes, but human! He who had come after her by chance or purpose had been in the right position to be scented. The sargon was after him.

She had sent this horrible death in that direction! Elossa felt cold flooding through her, following that realization. She had done the unthinkable, loosed death at a creature whose species she shared. Raski might be subjected to illusion, they could not be death doomed by Yurth. She had. . . . The horror of her act made her sick. For space of a breath she could not even think, just felt the terror of one loosing forces not to be controlled.

Then, snatching up her staff, leaving her bag of provisions where she had tossed it, Elossa turned back to the slope up which she had climbed. Hers the fault, if she went to death now it was no more than the payment she had so earned. That other had bow, wore steel—but neither could turn a sargon.

She slipped and slid, the skin of her hands scraped raw, intent on keeping her footing. No need to court a fall, which could serve nothing, save perhaps wipe out by death the memory of these past few moments.

Once more the sargon screeched. It had not yet closed in. But how much time had she? Her Yurth-trained mind began to shake free from the shock of knowing what she had done. To go down this way would avail her nothing. Her staff was no weapon with which to face what would be there. There was only . . . the rog!

Elossa struggled to marshal her thoughts, gather strength. She stood on a small ledge, her back to the rock of the mountain, looking down. The stubby brush of the lower slope hid what lay there.

Rog! Like a summons a battle commander might shout when hard pressed her thought leaped out. It caught that other animal mind, fighter the rog might be and was. Ferocious, it was not insane as was the sargon. Now she thrust with power where normally she would have inserted an idea slowly, gently. Sargon . . . here . . . hunting . . . kill . . . kill!

The other huge carnivore responded. Elossa played upon its hatred, bringing that emotion to a pitch which would have burned out a human mind entirely. The rog was on the move!

Out of the dusk came a second cry—and that was human!

She was too late—too late! Elossa gave a dry sob. Once more she began the descent. There was no more need for the rog to be goaded into battle. It was ready. Now she must seek the man who might be already dead.

Pain, yes, but he still lived. Not only lived but fought! He had climbed to a height where the sargon could not yet reach him. But that would not serve him as a refuge for long. Also he was wounded, easy meat for a furred monster now making a determined effort to pull him down.

Rog. . . .

As if in answer to that thought a third cry sounded. Now she saw. Across the slope, angling straight for the brush-hidden parts below, came a huge dark shape. Standing taller than she at the shoulder, its thick body so covered with dense fur that its short legs were nearly hidden, it scrambled, its claws loosing showers of small rocks, earth and gravel.

Even among rogs this was a giant, old enough to be a wary fighter, for only the strongest survived cubhood. It was indeed a fit match, perhaps the only one for the sargon. As it came it bellowed for a second time, sounding a challenge which, Elossa hoped, might draw the enemy from its final attack upon its victim.

The challenge was answered by a screech. Elossa swallowed. Would the sargon attempt to make sure of its prey before it turned to do battle? She sought to enter the raging mind. Rog! She was not sure that her mental prod did any good now. The mind of the thing was an insane whirl of death and the need for destruction.

Rog! Her urging might be futile, but it was all she could do. She was sure that the man yet lived. For a snuffed life was never to be mistaken. That she would have felt as a kind of diminishing of herself. Not such a blow as would issue from a Yurth death, still to be picked up.

The rog had halted, in a spray of gravel flying outward from its feet. Now it reared, to stand with its heavy forepaws, the huge claws visible against its dark fur, dangling. Its head, which appeared to be mounted on no neck but resting directly on its wide shoulders, raised so that the muzzle pointed in the direction of the brush, jaws slightly agape to show the double row of fangs.

Then, out of concealment came the sleek, narrow head of the sargon. The creature screeched once more, threads of foam dripping from its mouth. Long and narrow as a serpent, its body drew together as might a spring. Then it launched itself through the air directly at the waiting rog.

3

The beasts crashed together in a shock of battle which reached Elossa not only by sight and sound, but as an impact of raw emotion against her mind to nearly sweep her from her own feet before she was able to drop a barrier against it. Rog and sargon were a tangle of death-seeking blows. Elossa crept on hands and feet along the slope above to reach a point where she dared descend. Her duty still lay in that danger spot below. She was certain that he whom the sargon had attacked was wounded. The stab of pain her mind-seek had picked up had been enough of a jolt to suggest he might be in grave danger still.

She slipped downward until the brush closed about her; any sound she might make in that passage was well covered by the clamor of the battle. Once hidden by the growth she got to her feet, using her staff to hold back branches and open a way.

Very cautiously she sent out the thinnest of probes. To the left, yes, and down! Elossa was sure she had the position of the other centered. Shutting her mind against the emanations of rage beamed from the struggling animals, she went on.

The brush thinned out. She was in the open where rocks clustered under the rapidly growing dusk. Though she had closed her mind and the noise from above was ear-splitting, Elossa caught the moan of pain.

On the top of the highest of those rocks something half arose, to fall back again and lie, one arm dangling down the side of the stone. Elossa set her staff against a shorter outcrop of rock and scrambled up. There was still enough light to see the limp body with a spreading stain down left side and shoulder.

She moved cautiously, for his body near covered the top of the perch he had found as his only hope of life. Then she knelt beside him to examine a wound which had slashed downward from shoulder to rib, tearing away flesh as easily as one might peel the skin from a ripe fruit.

At her girdle was a small bag holding Yurth remedies. But first, though he had not moved at her coming, she knew she could not work while consciousness remained. Not only was intense pain a barrier to what she must do—and the Raski knew no form of inner control to that—but also she could not heal where a conscious mind could well impede her out of ignorance. Drawing a deep breath the girl sat back on her heels. What she *must* do (for this hurt was her work) went against custom and law of the Yurth. Yet the obligation laid upon her was also ruled by even higher law. What she had harmed, she must try to help.

Slowly, with deliberation and great caution, as she was engaged in a forbidden thing, one she was not trained for, Elossa began to insert her mind-send.

Sleep, she ordered, be at rest.

There was a response. His head jerked against her knee, his eyes half opened. She had touched something, yes. He was still on the borderland of consciousness and was partly aware of her invasion.

Sleep . . . sleep. . . .

That fraction of consciousness faded under deliberate mental command. Now she inserted another order, willing away pain. It was still there, yes, but like a far off thing. This she had done with animals found injured, with a Yurth child who had fallen and broken an arm. But the animals had trusted her, the child knew what she would do and was prepared to surrender to her. Would it also work for the Raski who looked upon her kind with hatred and suspicion?

Sleep. . . .

Elossa was sure he was past the threshold of consciousness. She could find in her delicate search no further alert against her invasion.

Now she drew her belt knife to cut away the rags of his leather jerkin, the shirt stiff with blood underneath that, laying bare a frightful wound which tore shoulder to hip. Out of her belt bag she took a folded cloth to spread flat upon her knee. Across it was a thicker layer of ground, dried herbs mixed with pure fat.

With infinite care she worked to bring together the

strips of torn flesh, holding them with one hand
while with the other she laid the cloth, bit by bit,
over the wounds. Though the blood had been flowing, yet, when that sealing cloth went on, there was
no more seepage. In the end the wound was covered
from end to end.

Elossa must release her mind-hold upon him now.
All her power and skill with the talent had to be
centered elsewhere. Slowly, as slowly as she had
entered his thoughts, she withdrew. Luckily he did
not rouse, at least not yet.

She laid her fingertips along the cloth. Focusing
her will, she built a mental picture of healing
flesh, clean healing. She must assume that Raski
bodies were not too different from those of the
Yurth. Blood, she commanded, cease to flow. Cells
she stimulated to begin growth of new connecting
tissue.

The drain of energy was such that she could actually feel it flowing out of her fingertips into the hurt.
Heal! Back and forth her fingers passed, touching
lightly the surface of the cloth, sending through that
the force of the Upper Sense aimed at this one task
alone.

She had reached the end of her endeavor, weari-
ness was about her as an outer skin. Her hands dropped
to her sides, her shoulders were bent. The dark had
now so enclosed them that she could not see the face
of the sleeping man save as a white blue. But he
slept, and for him she could do no more.

Elossa raised her head with a great effort. Now she
was aware that the clamor of battle was stilled. Her
concentration relaxed. She wanted to seek out through

the night, but the power was far spent, her whole body was so drained that she could not even move, only sat hunched beside the sleeper, waiting and listening in a dull way.

No sound. Nor did the feeling of aroused fury sweep toward her. She could not seek to penetrate the dark with mind-send. It might be a full day and night, or more, before she might draw back into her even a fraction of the talent she had used.

There was a sigh out of the night. Once more that head moved against her knee. Elossa tensed. She had paid her debt to the Raski but she did not believe that her care of him would in any way mitigate the inborn hatred of his kind for hers. Though she had nothing to fear from him in his present weakened state, still his emotions, if he roused fully, would shatter the peace and quiet she must have to recover her own necessary strength.

Very slowly she pushed away from the man. In spite of her great fatigue she knew that she must make an effort to get away, out of his sight. She slipped down from the rock perch, steadied herself against that while she picked up her staff.

With that to lean on, Elossa turned once more to the slope. Out of the veiling brush she caught the scent of blood, the reek of rog and sargon intermingled. There in the open rested a mass of torn fur, splintered bone, from which all life had fled. Here two monsters, equally matched, had fought to the death of both.

The girl pulled herself past that horrible battlefield, digging the staff in to support herself. There was the sound of sliding gravel, a hoarse clack of bird, a patter of feet. Scavengers were coming out of the night. None of that noisome crew need she fear. They would find a feast awaiting.

Up and up. She had to pause often to gather her forces and settle her will the firmer. But, at length, she came into the cup of grass and growth where the spring pool lay. Wavering over, she plunged her face and hands into the sharp chill of the water. Then she fumbled with her provision bag, hunger gnawing within her.

She drank from the stream, chewed food she hardly tasted, struggling to keep awake while she ate. At last she could battle no longer. Around her neck she settled the chain of the seeing disc and that she put by her ear. Though she did not know the reason or the method by which that worked, it was tuned to her personally alone, and, when she set it so, it would rouse her against the coming of any danger.

Thus protected as well as she could be in this wilderness, Elossa stretched out on the tough grass, her traveling cape about her. There was no time tonight for the daily meditation upon all happenings which was a part of Yurth training. Instead she dropped into almost instant slumber as she relaxed her conscious hold on her mind.

Dreams could warn, could instruct, were of importance. For long Yurth minds had investigated, recorded, shifted and judged dreams. They had learned to control them, to pick from perhaps a muddling and puzzling sequence of dream pictures a scrap here, a fragment there, which could be carried over into wak-

ing and there answer some question, or propose one
to be investigated in the future.

Elossa was very used to dreams, some vivid and
alive, some so tenuous they were floating wisps she
could not capture even with her training.

But. . . .

She stood on a road, a road of stone blocks fitted
together with expert precision and art. Smooth and
solid under her feet was that road. It wound on, arose
by expert engineering into heights, until her questing
eyes could no longer follow it. She began to move
along the road, headed toward those heights. Behind
her came another presence, but she could not look
over her shoulder, she only sensed that it followed
behind.

Her feet did not quite touch the surface of that
stone way. Rather, she swiftly skimmed above the
stones. Up and up the road led, and she went, it
followed behind.

Her feet did not quite touch the surface of that
stone way. Rather, she swiftly skimmed above the
stones. Up and up the road led, and she went, that
other always following.

Distances were lessened by the speed with which
she moved. Elossa thought that she must have come
a long way since she had first seen the road. Now she
was among the mountains. Mists clung to her body,
but with the road as a guide she could not lose her
way. She passed so swiftly that all around was a
blur. There was some need, some desperate need,
that she reach a point ahead, though, what was that
need and where lay that point, she could not understand.

There were no other travelers along the road. Save for that one who came behind, whose speed was less than hers so he did not catch up. But the urgency which filled her was shared by him also. This much she knew.

Up and up, and then came a pass with mountain walls rearing high and dark in either hand. When she stood in the pass the force which had carried her hither abruptly vanished. Below the mists clung and veiled the lower slopes, the road which lay farther on.

Then, as if a curtain had been drawn aside, those mists were pulled from immediately before her. She did indeed look down, and down, over such a drop as made her dizzy. Still she could move neither forward nor back.

Below were lights sparkling, as if a handful of cut gems had been spilled out. They shone from reaching towers, along walls, outlined great houses and buildings. This was a city far larger, far more majestic and imposing than any she had seen. The sweep of the towers was so marked that she thought at ground level they must seem to reach the sky.

There was life there but it was far away, dim in some fashion, as if another dimension besides distance lay between her and it.

Then. . . .

She heard no sound. But in the air there came a burst of flame as brilliant as an unshielded sun. This flame descended toward the city. Not to its heart, but at the far edge. The flaring outburst reached the wall there, spread over, to lick out at the nearest buildings.

Something hung above those flames. The fire sprouted from the bottom and a little up the sides of a dark globular mass. Down that came. The flames swept out, caught between the ground and the mass, fanning farther and farther.

She was too far away to see what must be happening to the city dwellers as this fate descended to crush and burn. Lights went out. She saw three towers break and fall as the mass riding the flames drew nearer. Then that rested part on the city, part without. Wall, tower, and buildings must have been crushed under it.

More flames arose, spreading farther over the city. Elossa wavered where she stood, fighting against the compulsion which held her there. In her there arose a keening sorrow, yet she could not give voice to the great sadness which tore at her. This castastrophe—it was not intended—but it happened and from it came a sense of guilt which made her cringe.

Then. . . .

Elossa opened her eyes. She did not stand in any pass watching the death of a city. No, she blinked and blinked again. For the space of several heartbeats she had difficulty in correlating the here and now with the then and there. There had carried over from the dream the sense of guilt, akin to that which had possessed her when she had realized that she had unwittingly sent death to stalk another.

The first of Zacar's twin moons was well up in the sky, its sister showing on the horizon. The beams silvered the water of the pool, made all within the cup of that small mountain meadow either shadow black or moon white. One of the scavenger birds croaked as it arose sluggishly from its feast.

Elossa settled into a deliberate pattern of even breathing to steady her nerves. That her dream had been one of the important ones she did not doubt. Nor did it begin to blur and fade from her mind after the fashion of most dreams. She had witnessed the destruction of part of a city. But the reason why she had been given this vision she did not know.

She took in her hands the seeing disc, being half minded to try a search. Did that city—or had it—ever existed here? Had that road she followed to the pass been the one time had nearly erased? She longed to know. Yet prudence counseled no, she must not again use her talent until she was sure within herself that she had an ample supply of energy.

Slowly she settled back, her hands crossed upon her breast under the folds of her cloak, and clasped in her right one the disc. But she did not fall again into slumber. The memory of her dream was like the dull aching of a tooth, prodding at her mind, plucking at her imagination.

Why and where, when and how? There was nothing in all the teaching she had absorbed from early childhood which suggested the existence of any such city, either past or present. The Yurth did not gather in large cities. Their life, to the outer eye, was primitive and rough. What they did inwardly was something very different. While the Raski, for all their liking to gather in towns and the city of the King-Head, had certainly produced nothing to equal what she had seen in her dream.

No, this was a mystery, and mysteries both drew and repelled her. Something lay within the mountains which was of importance—the very fact of the Pilgrimage testified to that. What would she find? Elossa looked upon the rising moon and strove to put her mind into the serene order demanded by her kind.

4

With the coming of day Elossa filled her water bottle, ate sparingly of her supplies, and began to climb again. The freshness of the mountain air drove away some of the shadow which had overhung the day before. There was only fleeting thought of the man below. She had done for him all that she could, the rest depended upon his own strength. To attempt to contact him now might betray herself and her mission.

On and on, the climb was a sharp one. She did not set a fast pace, conserving her energy by seeking out those places which were most easy to pass. Here the wind was chill. Already there were scarves of white snow along the upper peaks. Late summer, early autumn on the plains turned to winter here.

Once when she paused to rest, surveying curiously what lay about her, there was a quick flash of memory. Not too far ahead the rise of rock walls was such as she had seen before. She crouched on a narrow ledge she had been following because it gave good footholds and arose along the slope as if it had been chiseled there to offer a path.

However, this ledge was of natural formation. What lay beyond her perch came from the hands of men, or at least it had been built to answer the demands of intelligence equal to human. There stretched the remains of a roadway.

Surely this could be the same road she had seen leaving the foothills, while before it now lay the pass of her dream. Elossa hesitated. A dream of guidance, showing her where she must go? Or a dream of warning, to say this is not your path? She had no hint of which it might be. To try to learn she summoned the memory of the dream.

In that the road had not been a tumble of broken stone, but firm and whole. Though she had not actually trod upon it, yet it furnished her with a guide. Also a dream, for all the horror of the burning, dying city, had not seemed a threat to her. It *was* a sending, she decided. Though it had not been beamed by any one of her people, she would have recognized instantly the technique. Therefore. . . . A past shadow?

The theory and explanation of those was as familiar to her as her own name. Acts which aroused great emotion on the part of the actors could impress upon the scene of those acts pictorial representation of the events. These emanations might be picked up a long time later by any whose nature left them open to such reception. She had seen in the past the shadows of three of the King-Head's forces who had gone to their death from a rog attack. Yet those deaths had occurred generations before her own birth. And how much greater the death of a city would be—to imprint the agony of that loss upon the site!

Elossa dropped her head into her hands, forcing away the dream memory, reaching out for the compulsion tie which had brought her on the Pilgrimage. That was there, and it pointed her to the mountain gap! Gathering up her bag and staff, she descended to the ancient road and doggedly continued along that to the pass. She was no farther than the length of her staff along that way before she swayed, set her teeth grimly upon her lip.

Though she retreated behind a thought barrier, that was no safe refuge as far as emotion was concerned. It was as if she were now buffeted by unseen blows, all sent to force her into retreat. What lay here had no substance, but to approach was like forcing a way through a kneehigh swift current designed to sweep her from her feet.

More than wind flowed through the pass. Anger came, as deep and fierce as the mindless rage of the rog and the sargon, a cry for—for vengeance. Elossa was not aware that her progress became unsteady, that she reeled from one side of the way to the other.

Pulled forward, pushed back—it would seem that the forces here were near evenly balanced and she was the plaything of them both. But she did win forward, even though it was but a step, a half step, length at a time. Breath filled her lungs only in painful gasps. The entire world had narrowed to the broken road, and on that only a few lengths ahead.

Elossa fought. She was enmeshed now in those two forces she could sense that she dared not even attempt to free herself. No, this she must see until the end.

On and up. Her own breathing filled her ears. Pain looped around her ribs ever more tightly. She would plant her staff in some crack a little before her, and then, by main effort, drag herself to that spot, look ahead for another anchor.

Time itself left her. This might have been morning, or hours near sunset, one day or the next. Beyond and around her now flowed life and time. She was near spent with every step.

At last she stumbled into a pocket of absolute stillness. So quick was the cessation of those two forces which had used her as an arena that she collapsed against a rock, hardly able to keep on her feet.

The girl was only aware of the heavy pounding of her heart, the rasping sound of her breathing. She felt as emptied of strength as she had after she had expended the talent to aid the Raski hunter.

At length Elossa raised her head. Then that harsh, heavy breathing caught in her throat. She was not alone!

Her efforts had brought her to the other end of the pass. As in her dream, mist curdled on the down slope, cutting out all view of the way below and beyond. But, stark against that mist, fronting her. . . .

In spite of control Elossa uttered a cry of terror, fear welled in her. She clutched the staff which could be her only weapon. A length of wood to use against—*that?*

In form it was roughly human. At least it stood erect on two limbs, held two more before it. One of those was half hidden behind the oval of a shield

which covered it near throat to thighs. The other, a seared paw, still possessed enough charred bone of fingers to clasp a sword hilt. A skull, blackened by fire, to which strips of burnt flesh still clung here and there, was overshadowed by a helm.

It—it had no eyes left—yet it saw! Its helmed head was turned in her direction. Nothing, no one of her species who had been so burned could live! Yet this, this *thing* stood erect, the teeth of that horrible skull bared in what seemed to Elossa to be a grin of mockery, born from recognition of her own fear and loathing.

Nothing could live so! She drew several short breaths to steady her nerves. If this thing could not live (and reason came flooding back to her to make that assurance) then it was a thought form. . . .

The thing had moved. To her eyes it was three dimensional, as solid as the hand she herself raised in a gesture of repudiation. Thought form—from whose brain—and why? The shield had swung up to a position of defense, so now only the hollows of the skull's eye sockets appeared above its smoke-darkened rim. The sword was held steady. It was coming toward her. . . .

A thought form—if it followed the pattern of such things—then what it fed upon, to give it more and more solid substance, was her own fear and sickness. It was not alive—save in as much as it could build itself life out of her own emotions.

Elossa licked her lips. She had dealt with illusions all her life. But then she, or those of her kin, had built those. This was totally alien, born of a mind she could not understand. How then could she find the key to it?

It was an illusion! She caught and held that thought to the fore of her mind. Yet it moved toward her, its stained sword rising slowly, ready to cut her down. Every instinct urged her to defend herself with her staff as best she could. But to yield to that demand would be her loss.

Thought form . . . Beneath her first horror and revulsion another emotion stirred. Perhaps that had been born out of her dream. It was not the skeleton apparition before her which caused terror now. No, it was her memory of the destruction of the city which she had witnessed.

Some guard or warrior who had died there. But in whose memory had such a thing lingered to be thrown against her now? And why?

Guard, of course! A guard who had died at his post. Maybe not a thought form born of any living mind, but rather a lingering of pain and rage so great that it could be projected long after the brain which had given it birth was dead.

"It is over." Elossa spoke aloud. "Long over." Words, what had words to do with this? They could not reach the dead.

But this was only a projection, knowing that she was safe—safe. . . .

Gathering assurance about her as she might the billows of her journey cloak she stood away from the rock against which she had sheltered. The guard was only the length of a sword thrust from her now. Elossa stiffened herself against any flinching, any belief that this might do her harm.

She went forward, straight in the way the dead blocked. It was the most dreadful test she had ever faced. On, one step, two. She was up against the figure now. One more step. . . .

It was. . . . She stumbled as that wave of raw emotion filled her, ate into her confidence, her sanity. Somehow she was through, one hand to her head which felt as if it were bursting with utter terror, terror which was all filling, which overwhelmed her thoughts, left only sensation.

Elossa had walked through!

Now she looked back. There was nothing. It was even as she had guessed. Both hands on her staff, leaning on that as her legs felt so weak that they might give way under her at any moment, the girl tottered on into the wet embrace of the mist which cloaked the descent from the pass.

There were—sounds. Visual had been the first attack, audible was the second. Screams, faint as if from some distance, but not from any animal; rather the last cries of torment and overriding fear too great for any mind to face without breaking. Elossa wanted to cover her ears, to do anything which would shut out that clamor of the dying. But to do that was again to acknowledge that these projections had power over her. She. . . .

Elossa saw a stir within the mist, movement near the ground. She halted as a figure crawled into clear sight. This one went on all fours, had no shield nor sword. Nor were the signs of the fire anywhere on it.

Though its progress was that of a stricken animal, slow, painful, yet, it, too, was human. One leg

ended in a blob of crushed flesh from which seeped
blood to leave a broad trail upon the rocks. The head
was raised, forced back upon the shoulders as if the
crawler sought ahead of her some goal which was the
only hope of survival.

For this thing coming out of the fog was a woman,
the long hair, sweat plastered to temples, did not fall
forward enough to hide what ripped clothing displayed, while that clothing bore no resemblance to
the few scorched rags the guard had worn. Blood-
stained and torn though it was, it had been a close-
fitting body suit of a green shade, unlike any garment
Elossa had ever seen.

The crawling woman reached forward to draw herself on. Then her mouth opened in a soundless cry
and she fell, still striving to hold up her head, looking at Elossa. In her eyes there was such a plea for
aid that the girl wavered, almost losing control of her
own determination not to be misled.

The silent plea from the woman struck into Elossa's
mind. This was no figure out of nightmare, but rather
one to pluck at her pity in a way as deeply demanding of action as the fear generated by the guard had
been. There was a feeling of kinship between them.
Though this stranger was not of Yurth, or not of the
Yurth blood, Elossa knew.

Help, help me! Unspoken, faint, those words in
Elossa's head vocalized out of the emotion rising
swiftly to fill her. Help. Unconsciously she knelt,
stretched out her hand. . . .

No! She froze. Almost, this illusion had won!

To be caught in an illusion, the primary fear of the
Yurth choked her. She hid her eyes with her hand,

swayed to and fro. She must not yield! To do so was to surrender all she was!

But hiding her eyes was not the way. As she had done with the guard, she must face squarely this thing born from emotion, face it and treat it for what it was—nothing but a shadow of what once might have been. As the guard had been fed from her fear (and perhaps the terrors of others who had been drawn into this way before her) so would this other be fed by her pity and wish to aid. She must rein that in and not be moved.

Elossa got to her feet. The woman on the ground had raised herself a little, levering her body up with one arm, one hand planted palm down against the stone. The other hand she held out to the girl be-seechingly, her need open in her staring eyes, her mouth working vainly, as if she could not force out words, but needs must try.

As she had done with the guard the girl gathered her force of will and determination. Staff in hand she walked deliberately forward. Nor did she look aside from the woman, for such an illusion must be faced in its entirety and without flinching.

On . . . on. . . .

Once more she was engulfed in a flood of feeling, pain, need, fear, above all the plea for aid, for comfort. . . .

She was through, shaking, spent. Once more the mist closed about her as she pulled herself on, striving to shake from her that upheaval of emotion which had attempted to net her a second time and in another and, to her, more deadly fashion.

It was well that Elossa had the road for a guide here

as the mist was so blinding that otherwise she could have wandered from her path unknowingly. The badly broken way was sometimes hidden by slides of earth and rock, but ever, as she pushed ahead, she would find it again. Then the fog began to thin. She was coming out of that when again she halted, turned to face up slope, toward the pass now hidden from her.

That was not illusion! She had been only half consciously casting about with the mind-search to make sure that other things besides the illusions did not hide here. So she had touched another mind, instantly withdrew.

Who?

She must know, even if probing would reveal her to whatever lurked above.

With the extreme caution she must use, Elossa stood on the moisture-slicked rock where the fog condensed some of its substance in drops, and reached out. . . .

It was. . . . He! The Raski she had thought left far behind. Why had he followed her? In spite of the healing she had brought to his wound, he surely had not recovered enough to make such a journey easy. But there was no deception possible in the contact she made. This was the same mind she had touched before. He was here—above. . . .

And. . . . She felt the wash of his fear. The guard—he must be confronting the guard. Without any defense against illusion (for he could not have that by his very nature) how was he going to fare?

Elossa bit hard upon her lower lip. Before, she had been to blame in part for his hurt and therefore she was bound by her honor to come to his aid. This time the situation was different. He had chosen this path of his own free will, not through any control set by her. Therefore she was not responsible for what might issue from his folly.

5

Go forward, commanded logic reinforced by all her training from birth. Still Elossa lingered, unable to break that tenuous contact with the other's fear. Go forward! This is none of your concern. *This* you did not bring upon him. If he chose to come skulking behind, then he must face the result of his folly.

She forced herself to take one step, two, resolutely closing her mind to any more emanation, even though a buried part of her fought that decision. The last tatters of the mist drifted away; now she could see the country below.

And. . . .

Against all logic Elossa had expected to see what her dream had shown her—a city—the thing from the sky which had brought ruin to it. There was indeed the plateau which stretched near as wide as part of the plains she had crossed. At a far distance she could distinguish shadow shapes of other mountains.

This range must encircle as a wall on three sides, like arms curved out in protection.

There was no city as such. But when she sighted certain hollows and rises in the plateau (all now cloaked in withering grass) the girl knew that there lay long lost and forgotten ruins. There even arose piles of stones which might be the last vestiges of walls.

She turned her head a little to the north, to follow the winding of such a wall. What lay there was not in the city, rather farther away than her dream had shown it. Only a portion of it now arched above the surface, but a dome of top showed still. That was the thing which had descended from the heavens to wreak destruction here.

It was toward that that the Pilgrimage compulsion clearly drew her. The force of that was stronger, urging her to complete her journey as swiftly as she might.

Here the road angled along the wall of the mountain, taking a turn to the left. It was much broken, large portions of it shorn away by sideslips or avalanches. This path was not one for the unwary; one foot misplaced could send her sliding to destruction.

Elossa concentrated all her attention on that descent, taking care, her staff often an anchor over a treacherous bit of path. The journey was longer than she had thought when she had viewed her goal from the heights.

So the sun was well up and it was midday before she reached the level of the plateau. There she paused to eat and drink before she turned from those grass-matted stones toward the dome.

Just as the trail had been longer than she had expected, so now did the ruins loom larger. In many places the mounds topped her head. While from their mass below a chill wind which made her wrap her cloak more tightly about her.

As the ruins had grown taller so did the curve of the buried globe rise higher. In her dream the whole globe had been great enough to blot out a goodly portion of the city; now she could understand how. Judging by the dream, all which remained above the soil now was perhaps a quarter of its entire bulk. Still that stood as high as perhaps three of the Raski dwellings set one atop another to form a tower.

It was uniformly gray in color, not the gray of a natural rock, but lighter, resembling the hue of the sky before the approach of a summer rainfall. As Elossa moved toward it a sighing of wind, blowing through the ruins, produced an odd wailing note. Dared she loose her fancy she could believe that filled with the far-off keening of voices lamenting the dead.

No, she had had enough of illusion! Elossa paused long enough to tap one of the half-buried stones with the end of her staff. It was satisfyingly solid under that contact—no illusion. Wind often had its own voice when it blew around and through rock formations, whether those were natural or man-made.

As she went the ruins grew yet higher, threw their own broken-edged shadows here and there. She found that she must alter her path and go farther in among those mounds in order to reach her goal. Doing so made every nerve shrink, protest.

Death—this was the way of death.

For a long minute the very air curdled, became a curtain, drew apart. She saw shapes with more substance than the mountain mist, still they might have been born of that. One such shape fled, the others were hounds behind it, wisps of arms raised. . . . While the shape which fled dodged and turned. . . . There was that in her which answered to it, knew the fear and torment which possessed it.

No! At once she clamped down her mind barrier. The shapes were gone, but Elossa never doubted that once such a hunt had crossed the path she must now follow.

Her energy had been drained, more than was normal, even though she had made that perilous descent of the mountain. She found she must lean more and more on her staff, even pause and rest, breathing fast to draw air into her lungs. She, too, might have been running at the desperate speed of that fog thing.

Her head jerked. The sensation that had come out of the air might have an unexpected blow, pulling her to the left. Now she saw a path winding westward among the mounds. In spite of her efforts at control the ordering of her own body was mercilessly rift from her. She turned, not by her will, but by a compulsion strong enough to override that other she had followed so far and long.

Elossa fought with every weapon of the Upper Sense she could summon. But there was no winning of this battle. She moved along that faint path, pulled by a cord she could not break. Still she also was very much aware that this was nothing of Yurth spinning— rather a contact totally alien to all she knew.

On she went. Now she no longer struggled to

break free. The caution in which she had been drilled suggested that both her will and strength might be put to a stronger test in the immediate future and it was well to conserve them now.

The mounds of ruins grew ever larger, loomed over her, shutting out the view of the half-buried dome, sometimes closing off all but a ribbon of sky well over her head. It was in such circumstances that the path ended in a dark opening at the side of one of the mounds. Seeing that ahead and guessing full well that whatever (or whoever) drew her intended that she enter that threatening doorway, Elossa braced herself for a final struggle. So intent was she on marshalling her forces, that she was unaware of what crept behind her.

There came a blow, landing to numb her shoulder so that she dropped her staff. Before she could turn or disengage thought power to defend herself, a light burst in her head and she fell forward into dark nothingness.

Sounds first aroused her from that nothingness. There was the deep tone which made the very air vibrate, and that came at spaced intervals. Her body answered to that beat, quivering as the tone slowly died away, shrinking before the coming of the next deep sound. It was so hard to think again.

Elossa opened her eyes. No sky, no daylight. Here was dark, battled only feebly by a flickering of flame she could see from eye corner. Always that beat of sound enwrapped her, keeping her off balance as she strove to use mind-touch, discover where she might be and who had brought her here.

Now the girl strove to move her body, but she

could not stir. She was not held in mind-thrall—very real bonds entrapped her. Rings prisoned her wrists, her ankles, a large one about both her legs at slightly above the knee level, and one binding her breast. She was fastened to a hard surface over which she moved fingertips, to learn she lay on stone.

The pound of the sound ceased. Elossa turned her head toward the light. That issued from a lamp, the metal of which was wrought in the form of a monstrous creature sitting up on hind quarters, while the light within it streamed from open mouth and eyes.

So limited was the range of that radiance she could not see beyond the lamp. There lay a darkness as thick as the mist had been in the mountains. However, with that overpowering beat at last stilled, she found that she could gather strength enough to send forth a mind-probe.

The Raski!

There would be no question now of what she must do. Those on the Pilgrimage were pledged and conditioned that nothing must interfere with their quest. Successful accomplishment of such was needful to the Yurth as a whole, for each one who made it and returned added new vigor and strength to the clan. She, herself, had felt that inflow of shared power on past occasions when the Pilgrimage feast was given after a return.

She *must* complete what she was sent to do. If her success meant the taking over of this inferior and "blind" mind, then that she would do also.

Having located her quarry, Elossa used a strong probe to follow the light contact she held. And. . . .

What she found made her gasp. A layered mind—a

double life lying side by side! The one which she
sought to reach was guarded by the other. Guarded,
or in thrall to? That was only a guess, however,
something impressed her that the full truth might well
be so.

But the Raski had no mind control, none of the
Upper Sense! What stronger mind could be here? She
dismissed at once the belief that another Yurth was
present. Not only was it against all custom, except in
the most dire occasions (such as the one she faced),
but what she had probed in the quick instant before
her snap of withdrawal had not been Yurth. Nor was
it Raski to the extent of the man who had followed
her. The possessor was another—another species?

She marshalled her defense, expecting a fierce
return probe which would have been natural under
the circumstances. What the Raski feared the most
was not the tangible weapons a Yurth held but had
discarded, rather the mind-send which the plains people considered unnatural and a kind of evil magic.
Only now there came no return stroke. Nor did the
Raski either move or speak.

Slowly once more Elossa sent out a tendril of
mind-seek, not a strong probe, more like a scout sent
to estimate the forces of the enemy. The Raski was
quiet in body, in mind she touched a seething of
force. Hate and vengeance—such as the illusion guard
had broadcast on the mountain. A hate which had
passed beyond the point of any reason. To all purposes the Raski was now mad, or rather held in the
grip of a madman's thoughts.

There were those among the Yurth who could
enter into the chaos now whirling in that other mind,

bring to it the peace of unconsciousness, until the cause for its trouble could be remedied. But those were old in learning and far more powerful than she.

Elossa dared not maintain contact for more than an instant or so at a time, lest she be caught in that mad whirl of hate and lack of logic, infected in turn. She could not be sure of what she dealt with now. This matter of two different personalities which she was sure were present was unlike ordinary mental imbalance.

She could only continue to pick delicately, striving to find a way into the personality she knew from the mountain trail, discovering a path past the other to reach that. To so strengthen the man she had touched earlier might be a way to defeat the mad thing which had settled into his mind.

Hate, that was like a fire fanned into her face, burning her mind as real flames could reduce her flesh to that which still clung to the charred skeleton of the pass.

No! Do not think of the guard, such memories strengthened the mad thing. As did the illusion form, it could feed on such a memory, grow stronger. Was that what happened to the Raski? Had he made contact with the thought form, and in some way absorbed thereby what rode him now?

Do not speculate! There was not time for anything but to marshal her will against an invasion of hate and fear. Elossa stared up into the darkness over her, unable to see the Raski to focus upon him. She reluctantly withdrew mind-touch lest that other use her own bridge as a path for counterattack.

Emotion charged this space in which she lay securely captive. It pressed in upon her like the beat of the sound which had drawn her from unconsciousness.

She had done nothing to give rise to such loathing. No, that reached from the past, the far past. And it had fed on fear for a long time. Now it was feeding upon the Raski, and it would feed on her also—unless she could hold her guard against it—for a space.

In the dark above her formed a head, the charred bone head of the guard. Skeleton jaws opened: Not with her ears but her mind she heard a cry:

"Death to the sky devils! Death!"

Elossa stared back at the illusion. It began to fade, its jaws still moving to mouth the soundless words. She did have a tie with the Raski who lent his strength, willingly or unwillingly, to this manifestation. Her healing had gone into his body, she had touched his flesh, sending into him the force which was hers to give.

Deliberately she closed her eyes. With one portion of the Upper Sense she kept watch for any sly attack on the mind-touch level. With the rest she began to build an illusion of her own, concentrating into it most of her strength. She had never tried this action before, but when one is faced with a new form of danger one must accordingly change one's defense.

Slowly her eyes opened. There was movement in the air above her where the death's head had hung. But this was her doing. As a worker with colored clay might project upon a stone wall some vision which had before lain only in his mind, Elossa built upon the air the form of her illusion.

There stood the rock on which she had found the Raski, firm and sturdy, gaining solidity with every breath she drew. On it now her imagination, well harnessed and schooled, laid the body of the Raski as she had seen him, the torn flesh, the freely running blood. Then she brought herself into the scene to straightway relive those moments when she had fought to save his life, using all the skills she knew. It was clear, that picture.

As the woman in the vision worked, so did Elossa gather up within her the emotion which such a healer uses—sympathy, pity, the wish for skill to aid what she would do. All the emotions naturally opposed to that burning hate. In the vision she labored to save a life, not blast it.

So, as was always true, emotion fed emotion. The woman strove as she had done to aid the man. Now Elossa turned her head to face the corner in which he lurked. The woman in the vision arose—her hand rested on her breast and then moved outward, as if bestowing some gift freely and gladly. From the outstretched hands of that illusion Elossa strove indeed to make sympathy and good will speed to the one who crouched in the dark.

6

The girl continued to beam a sense of healing and that good will with all her strength. In return came only the flame of the mad rage rising higher as if it were fed anew. She could no longer hold her pictured illusion. It winked out as might a lamp puffed by the wind. But the emotion which it had contained she still broadcast.

Friend . . . aid . . . peace . . . freedom from hurt and pain . . . Her whole being was absorbed in sending forth that message.

There was only the very dim lit space above her, empty of any illusion. Into that came a head—not building up slowly as had the skull of her own vision. So dim was the lamp by her side that she could see only half a face, and that was drawn into a grimace which resembled the rictus of the dying.

No vision. This was the Raski who had shuffled to her side, and now stood looking down at her. She saw the working of his mouth, the one eye staring dully in the lamp light.

Peace . . . peace. . . .

A hand came into view, its fingers crooked into the form of talons, held about her as if to rake the flesh from her bones.

Peace—there is peace between us. . . .

That hand wavered, clawed down at her, the nails scraping feebly at her tunic. There was little of the human in the face. Elossa was tempted to use the probe, thought better of it. That which possessed this man was alert to what she did. There could be no hope of a victory fighting on its level. She must rather hold fast to her own, perhaps ineffectual, way of counterattack.

Peace—peace between us, man of the Raski. No harm from me—I have tended your wound, perhaps given you life. Peace between you and me now— peace!

His hand relaxed, fell to lie limply on her breast. Another form of contact! Such could carry a greater charge than thought alone. Now his head bent forward farther into the light. The terrible mad grin which had stretched his mouth began to ease away. That dull stare of the eye which was completely visible changed. Deep in it, she was sure, shone a measure of intelligence.

Elossa gathered all her force for a final attack upon the thing buried in him.

Peace! Though the word was but thought, it held all the power of a shout.

His head jerked as it might from a blow in his face. Now that eye closed, his features went utterly slack as he fell across her, his weight pressing her painfully against the stone on which she lay.

Elossa tried the probe. The rage had drained out of him, or else it had been pushed so deep that she could not reach him without giving that insanity a new gateway to the surface. He lay unconscious— open. Now she could do what would give her an only chance.

Into that open mind she beamed a command. His body arose by degrees, not easily, rather as if he resisted her even though he had no control. She had implanted a single order, and that with all the strength left in her.

Wavering, he swung away from her sight. She thought from a faint sound he must have gone to his knees beside the slab she was prisoned on. There came a metallic sound like unto the click of a shot bolt, the turn of some reluctant locking device. The bands which held her slipped away and she sat up.

The Raski huddled beside that table (or perhaps it was an altar of sacrifice; she suspected that the latter was the truth). He did not stir to impede her as she slipped over the edge of the opposite side and stood up, feeling stiff and sore as if her ordeal in that place had lasted longer than she knew.

But she was unharmed and she was free! Though how long? If she went on her quest a second time, leaving him behind, what was the chance that he would not again be claimed by the spirit which had used his body to bring her down? Very great, Elossa thought. Therefore she dared not go and leave him behind, little as she wanted to take him with her.

She was again breaking custom and the Law of her

clan to contemplate such action, yet she could see no choice other than killing a helpless man. That deed would bring on her such a burden of wrong doing that she would be changed irrevocably into someone who could never more be any but an outcast wanderer.

Rounding the table she caught the Raski's head between her two hands, turned his face up into the dim light. The eyes were open, but without any spark of intelligence in them. His features seemed oddly shrunken as if some portion of his life force had drained away.

Elossa drew upon all remnants of her will. There were only remnants now, for the ordeal of her battle with the mad thing had near exhausted her. Holding him so, and looking down into his unseeing eyes, she loosed that which remained of her drained will in a second sharp command.

His body stirred. She held him fast for several breaths more, giving to this all she had left. Then, as she stepped back, he put his hands on the edge of the table altar. Bracing himself against that he got to his feet, stood, his blind eyes on her, his arms now dangling loosely by his sides.

Then he turned, stumbling. On into the dark beyond the reach of the lamp he lurched, Elossa after him.

It would seem that this thick dark did not hinder him. She caught at one of the dangling tatters of the jerkin she had cut away from his body to tend his wound. With that tugging in her hand she could not lose contact.

She thought that they were transversing a passage underground, for a dank smell filled her nostrils. Then that ribbon of leather which united them pulled upward at a new angle. A moment later her toes stubbed against a step.

Up he climbed and she followed. The dark so pressed in upon them that it was an almost tangible thing. What if her hold on the Raski's mind failed while they went this way, and the madness would possess him again here in the blackness? No, do not even think of that, for such thoughts could perhaps unloose in turn just that which she must keep at bay.

On and up—until at last they came to another level hallway. Ahead Elossa saw a grayish glimmer which gave her an instant of excitement and triumph. That must be a door to the outer world!

The Raski went more and more slowly. She read his reluctance. Still she did not try mind contact again. A probe, no matter how delicately used, could well break her hold on him.

They emerged from the fetid and musky darkness into the gray light of early day. Around them hunched the mounds, dark and menacing, like rog and sargon waiting to pull down those who invaded their jealously held territory.

With these so tall about her Elossa was not sure in what direction stood the dome which had drawn her here.

For a moment she hesitated. The Raski wavered on, free of the hold she had kept upon him in the dark ways. He did not turn his head or show any awareness of her. Elossa, with no better guide, came behind.

The mounds ceased abruptly to exist. Here instead was a section where the only signs of the one-time city were lines on the ground. Then even those ceased to be, and they were out in the open transversing an empty space.

Looming above was the dome, its surface dull in this subdued light. The Raski stopped short. His hands came up with one swift movement to cover his eyes. It could be that he refused to look upon the structure ahead, that it implied a threat to which he had no answer.

Elossa caught him by the upper arm. He did not drop his hands nor look at her. Though when she strove to draw him on he resisted her feebly. She had to guide him for he did not change the position of that blindfold of flesh and blood he had raised.

So they came to the foot of the dome. Elossa dropped her hold on her companion. Now. . . . She licked her lips. Though she had not been told what she would find here, she had carried one aid in the quest. She had been given a single word and told that when the time came for its use she would know it.

The time was here—and now.

Raising her head high, the girl fastened her eyes upon the swell of the dome and cried aloud.

There was no meaning in the word-sound—at least none that she knew. The sound itself re-echoed in the air about her.

Then came the answer. First with a harsh grating as if long rusted or deep set metal moved against bonds laid by time. On the surface of the dome, well above her, appeared an opening. That continued to enlarge until wide enough to admit a body. From that doorway sounded another complaint of metal, continuing, as there issued out a curving strip like a tongue aimed to lick them up.

Elossa retreated warily, drawing the Raski with her. The tongue of metal, which had issued with such effort, now curved down, touched end to earth a little to her right. She saw that it was a stepped way. So was she bidden to enter.

Again she dared not release the man with her. What lay within the dome must be the great mystery of the Yurth. But to allow this one free, perhaps waiting as a receptacle for returning madness, would be like setting a weapon edge to her own throat.

She laid hands on him once more only to meet stronger resistance. He voiced a word in a voice so faint that it might have come from a far distance:

"No!"

As she pushed him to the foot of the ladder ramp, wondering how she could force him to climb if he set all his strength against her, he cried out, to be echoed hollowly:

"Sky devil! No!"

However, he was still subject enough to her mind-command that he could not escape and so began to climb, every tense line of his body arguing his struggle to be free. They went slowly. Elossa could see nothing beyond that opening. Nor did she try to use the mind-search to learn what might await them there.

For now she was aware of something else; around her gathered and grew that mad hate she had twice faced and which now began a third assault. The Raski suddenly threw back his head, lifting his face to the sky. He howled, mouthing a cry which held no human note in it.

She feared he would break the mental bond, turn and rend her with the brainless ferocity of a sargon.

But, though he howled once more and his fear and rage enveloped her, still her will subdued that in him which struggled for freedom and he continued to climb.

They came to the door. The Raski flung out both arms, caught at the sides of that portal, bracing his body as if this were his last stand against unnamable terror and despair.

"No!" he screamed.

Elossa, now afraid that he would swing around, throw her down the incline of that ramp-ladder, did not wait to send a mind-probe. Instead she thrust vigorously, her hands sriking him waist high. Perhaps the speed of that physical attack made it successful. He stumbled, his head falling forward on his chest. Then that stumble continued and he crumpled, to lie motionless.

Elossa squeezed past him, turned and stooped, hooked her fingers in the belt which held his torn clothing to his body. Exerting her strength, she pulled him well into the hall.

Then. . . .

Instinctively she braced her body as one preparing for defense. For out of the air—not in her mind, but rather in words she could understand, though they had a different accent from true Yurth speech—there came a message.

"Welcome, Yurth blood. Take up the burden of your sin and shame and learn to walk with it. Go forward to the place of learning."

"Who are you?" Her voice was shaken, thin. There came no answer to her question. Nor would there be, some sense within her knew.

The Raski rolled over on the floor, lay staring up at her. There was no cloudiness in his eyes now, rather a fierce, demanding intelligence. He pulled away, to sit up, looking about him as a trapped animal might search for a way out of a cage.

From the doorway sounded once more the scraping of metal. The Raski whirled but he did not even have time to get to his feet. Inexorably the door slid shut, they were sealed into this place.

"Where are we?" He used the common tongue forged between Raski and Yurth.

Elossa answered with the truth. "I do not know. There was a city . . . in ruins . . . but that you know. . . ." She watched him carefully. It was true that sometimes some inner safeguard could wipe from memory all trace of the immediate past—if that memory threatened the well-being of the mind. To her ear his bewilderment suggested this might have happened to him.

He did not answer at once. Instead he surveyed what lay about them, the smooth walls which stretched away to form a narrow hall, no break in them. He frowned as his gaze returned to her.

"City—" he repeated. "Do not tell me we are in Coldath of the King."

"Another place, older, far older." She thought that the King-Head's capital which he named might have been lost in this place when it had been a home for men.

He put his hand to his head. "I am Stans of the House of Philbur." He spoke to himself, she knew, rather than to her, reassuring himself of his own identity. 'I was hunting and. . . ."

His head came up again. "I saw you pass. I was warned that when any Yurth sought the mountains I must be prepared to follow. . . ."

"Why?" she asked, disturbed and surprised. This was a breaking of an old tradition and had an ominous sound.

"To discover whence comes your devil-power," he replied without hesitation. "There was . . . surely there was a sargon." His hand went to his side where her plaster still clung to his flesh. "That I did not dream."

"There was a sargon," Elossa assented.

"And you tended this." His hand continued to rest upon his side. "Why? Your people and mine are ever unfriends."

"We are not unfriends enough to watch a man die when we might aid him." There was no need to explain her own part in his wounding.

"No, you are content to be murderers!" He spat the words into her face.

7

"Murderers?" Elossa echoed. "Why do you name us that, Stans of the House of Philbur? When has any of the Yurth brought death to your people? When your King-Head came hunting us, swearing to kill us all, man, woman, child, we defended ourselves, not with drawn steel, but with illusion which clouds the mind for a space, yes, but does not kill."

"You are the Sky Devils." He arose, bracing his shoulders against the wall of that hall, facing her as a man might face great peril when his hands were empty of any weapon.

"I do not know your sky devils," she returned. "Nor do I mean any harm to you, Stans. I have come hither by the custom of the Yurth and for no reason which means ill to you and yours." She was eager to get on, to obey the voice which had welcomed her here. That compulsion which had led her to the mountains, and, in turn to the dome, had become an overwhelming urge to go on to some inner place which would show to her what she must learn.

"The custom of the Yurth!" His mouth moved as if he would spit upon her even as had the girl in the town. Anger blazed out of him, but it was not that madness which had controlled him in the ruins. This was natural and not the result of possession.

"Yes, the custom of the Yurth," Elossa returned quietly. "I must complete my Pilgrimage. Do I go in peace to do that? Or is it that I must set mind-bonds upon you?" She believed that she really could not do so. Her energy was far too sapped by what she had called upon to aid her in escape. But she must not let him realize that, and she knew that, above all else, the Raski feared mind-touch for any reason.

However, she could not read any fear in him now. Had he realized in some manner that her threat was an empty one?

"You go." He stood away from the wall. "I also come."

To refuse him would mean a confrontation either at mind level (which she was very dubious about winning) or on the physical plane. Though her thin body could endure much, the thought of such a contact by force was one any Yurth would find revolting. Touch, except for very special reasons and at times when one was completely relaxed, no Yurth could long endure.

She did not know what lay before her; that it was an ordeal, a testing of her kind she did not doubt. What might it be for a Raski intruder? She could envision traps, defenses against one of another race or species which could slay—either mind or body or both. All she could do was warn.

"This is a sacred place of my people." She used the term which he must understand. Though the Yurth had no temples, worshipped no gods that had any symbols, they recognized forces for good and evil, perhaps too removed from human kind to be called upon. The Raski did have shrines, though what gods or goddesses those harbored the Yurth neither knew nor cared. "Do your temples not have sites of Power which are closed to unbelievers?"

He shook his head. "The Halls of Randam are open to all—even to Yurth, should such come."

She sighed. "I do not know what barriers for a Raski may be raised here. I warn, I cannot foresee."

His head was held proudly—high. "Warn me not, Yurth woman! Nor believe that where you go I fear to follow. Once my House dwelt in Kal-Nath-Tan." He made a gesture toward the door through which they had come. "Kal-Nath-Tan which the sky-devils slew with their fire, their wind of death. It is told in the Hearth-room on my clan house that we once sat in the High Seat of that city and all within raised shield and sword when they cried upon our name. I am the last to bear the sword and wear the name that I do. It would seem that Randam has ordained that I be the one to venture into the heart of the sky-devil's own place.

"Other men of the clan have come seeking. Yes, we have followed Yurth hither. One in each generation has been bred and trained to do so." He stood away from the wall, straight and tall, his pride of blood enwrapping him as might the state cloak of the

King-Head. "This was my *geas* set upon me by the very blood within my veins. Galdor rules in the plains. He sits in a village of mud and ill-laid stone. While his House of Stitar was even not numbered in the shrine of Kal-Nath-Tan. I am no shieldman of Galder's. We of Philbur's blood raise no voice in his hall. But it is said in the Book of Ka-Nath which is our treasure: there shall rise a new people in the days to come and they will rebuild what once was. Thus we have sent the Son of Philbert each generation to test the worth of that prophecy."

Oddly he seemed to grow before her eyes, not in body but in that emanation of spirit to which the Yurth were sensitive. This was no hunter, no common plains dweller. There was that in her which recognized a quality which she had not been aware any Raski possessed. That what he said he believed to be the truth she did not question. Nor was it beyond possibility. The very fact that he had been so possessed by the hatred and need for vengeance which hung like a cloud of swamp fog here could be because of some ancient blood tie with the long dead.

"I do not deny your courage, nor that you are of the blood of those who once dwelt in this place you give name to, but this is Yurth." She gestured to what lay about them. "Yurth may have set defenses. . . ."

"The which may act against me," he interrupted her quickly. "That is true. Yet it is set upon me—a *geas* as I have said—that I must go where the Yurth who comes here goes. Never before has one of us been able to penetrate within this place. Yurth has died, and so have those of the House of Philbur, but none of my clan have won so far. You cannot keep me from this now.''

She could, Elossa thought. It was plain that this Raski did not understand the breadth and depth of Yurth mind control. Only in her at this moment there was not enough strength to take him over or immobilize him against his will. She schooled herself against any concern. He swore he would do this thing; very well, let any ill results from his folly be upon his own head. This time she was in no manner to be held in blame.

Elossa turned and started down the hall. She was aware, without turning to look, that Stans followed. It was time to forget about him, to concentrate all which remained of her near-exhausted Upper Sense on what lay ahead.

She opened her mind fully, waiting to pick up a guide. Elossa fully expected to find such, but nothing came in reply to her questing. The dome might be as sterile and dead as the ruins her companion had named Kal-Nath-Tan. The hall ended in what appeared to be blank wall.

Still this was the only way and she must follow it to the end. However, as she was still a step or two away from that dead end, the wall broke open along a line she had not seen, a part of it moving to her left and leaving the way open.

There was a light within this place which came from no bowl lamp or torch, rather from the ways themselves. So now she did not face darkness, rather a well in which a stair wound around to a center pole. Part of it went down, the rest climbed to disappear through a hole above. Elossa hesitated and then made her choice to go up.

The climb was not too long, bringing her out in a room where she stood looking around her with a heart which suddenly beat faster. This chamber was totally unlike the bare caves of the Yurth or their summer-time huts of woven branches, just as it was different from the squat, dull dwelling of the Raski.

It was not bare. Around the circular walls stood set boards covered with opaque plates. Before these, at intervals, were seats. While one section of the wall itself was a huge plate, much larger than all the rest, confronted by two seats side by side. Directly behind these twin seats was a taller one of such importance that it drew her eyes in a compelling way.

Hardly knowing why she did, Elossa crossed to stand with her hand resting on the back of the chair. Her touch alerted at last what she had been seeking—a guide. Once more there rang the deep "voice" which had greeted their entrance.

"You of Yurth, you have come for the knowledge. Be seated and watch. No longer shall one of you look upon the stars which were once your heritage, now you shall see rather what was wrought on *this* world and what part those of your blood played in it. For it was recorded and it comes from out of memory banks—that you may learn. . . ."

Elossa slipped into that throne-like seat. Before her stretched the wide screen. Now she collected her whirl of thought.

"I am ready." But she was not; there was a rising sense of something far more potent than uneasiness, this was the beginning of fear.

On the opaque screen before her there was a flicker of light which spread out from a center point to cover the plaque. The light vanished. She looked out upon a vast stretch of darkness in which there were only a few clusters of tiny, brilliant points.

"The star ship Farhome, in the colony service of the Empire, Year 7052 A.F." Impersonal that voice, with nothing of human in it. "Returning from placing a colonial group on the third planet of the Sun Hagnaptum, three months out in flight from base."

A star ship! Elossa licked her lips. Stars there were to be seen, yes. Also she had been taught that far away and small as they looked in the night sky, they were in truth suns, each perhaps with worlds, such as this on which she now stood, locked in patterns of orbit about them. But never had it been suggested to her that man might actually cross the vast void of space to visit another of those planets.

"On the fifth time cycle," continued the voice, "there was radar contact made with an unknown object. This was identified as an artifact of unknown origin."

On the surface of the picture before her came into view a small object which grew quickly larger and larger, leaping toward the screen she watched until she involuntarily flinched.

"Evasive tactics proved valueless. There was crippling contact made. A quarter of the crew of the Farhome were killed or injured by that encounter. It was necessary to set down on the nearest planet, since the matter transferrer was completely wrecked.

"There was a planet just within range which offered a possible refuge."

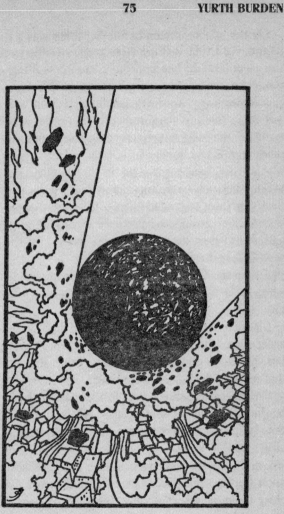

Now a globe snapped into view, grew larger and larger, until first it filled the screen, and then continued to enlarge in one portion, Elossa could see, until mountains and plains were thoroughly visible.

"A site away from any inhabited section was chosen for a landing. Unfortunately there was a human error in the data given the computer control. The landing was ill-chosen."

Another change appeared in the picture. Rushing toward her now were mountains, cupping a piece of level territory. Situated there—the city! Surely that was, though strange when viewed from the air above and so, to her, out of focus, the same city she had seen in her dream.

Faster and faster the picture produced more details, spread out farther. They were coming down on the city! No!

Elossa cried that aloud and heard her voice ring around the chamber. Fire spread outward in a great fan, bit down into the city. Then all was fire, and, in that instant, the screen went dead.

"More of the ship's people were killed by a bad landing," the voice continued. "The ship itself could not be raised from where it had crashed. The city. . . ."

Once more the screen came alive and Elossa looked upon horror. She could not even control her eyes to close them against that view. Fire—the impact of the globe ship itself—death spread outward from where it had set down.

"The city," continued the voice, "was slain. Those who survived were in shock. All they had left was mad hatred for what had been done to them. They were warped, maddened by the blow. Their condition was an infection, a disease."

Elossa witnessed, unable to turn away, other terrors. The issuing forth of the ship's people to try to aid, their hunting down and slaying by the insane natives. Then came degeneration of those natives, eaten by a trauma which spread outward from the dead city, infecting all that came in touch with its fleeing people, the fall of a civilization.

The people of the ship, the handful that remained, gathered together, accepted the burden of the wrong they had done. Though it was the fault of only one, yet they took upon them all the responsibility. The girl saw them using certain machines within the ship, deliberately turning upon themselves a power she could not understand, resulting in the punishment they sought. Never again could those so treated by the machines hope to rise to the stars. They were earthbound on the world they had ravished, whose people they had broken.

However, from the use of the machines which forbade them flight there came something else. Within them awoke the Upper Sense, as if some mercy had been so extended to lighten the burden of their exile.

"There is a reason for everything," the voice continued. "As yet Yurth blood have not found the final path they must walk. It is laid upon them never to stop the seeking. It may be given to you, who have made the Pilgrimage now, to find that path, to bring into light all those who struggled in the darkness. Search—for some time there will be such a discovery."

The voice was still. Elossa knew without being

told that it would not speak to her again. There flowed in upon her such a sense of loss and loneliness that she cried out, bowed her head to cover her face with her hands. Tears flowed to wet the palms of those hands. It was such a loss which even the death of someone she was kin to could not equal. For among the Yurth there were no close ties, each was alone within himself, locked, she saw now, in a prison she had never understood before. Until this moment she had accepted this loneliness without being aware of it. That, too, the machine which had awakened the Upper Sense had left with them as dour punishment.

She could feel now, deep in the innermost part of her a glimmering of need. What need? Why must the punishment be laid upon them over and over, generation after generation? What was it that they must seek in order to be entirely free? If not to reach the stars from which they had been exiled, then here, that they need not always walk apart—even separate always from their own kind?

"What must we do?" Elossa dropped her hands, and stared at the dark and lifeless screen. She had not used mind-speech, her demand had been aloud, delivered to the dead silence of the room.

8

Elossa did not expect any answer. She was certain she would never hear that voice again. Whatever result might come from this widening of her knowledge would be born from her thoughts and actions alone. Slowly she arose from the chair. Just as the Upper Sense had been drained by her exertions to reach this end of her quest, so now was hope and belief in the future ebbing from her.

What was left for the Yurth? They, whose blood had once dared the star ways, were planted forever on a world which hated them—outcasts and wanderers. Of what purpose were they? Better that they take steps now to erase their existence. . . .

Bleak and bitter thoughts, yet they clung to her mind, made the world look gray and cold.

"Sky-devil!"

Elossa turned to meet the eyes of the Raski. She had forgotten him. Had he seen what she had been forced to witness, the destruction of the world which had been that of his blood and kin?

She held up her hands, empty and palm out. "Did you see?"

Had the pictures on the screen been for her alone, cast there by a mental force denied his kind?

Now he tramped forward. The madness did not haunt his eyes, he was all man, not possessed by any emanation from the dead. His face was sternly set— and she could no longer use a mind probe to read his thoughts! It was as if he, too, had one of the barriers the Yurth could set about them.

"I saw." He broke the small moment of silence which had fallen. "This—" He slapped the back of the chair in which she had sat with force enough to make it quiver a little as if it were not firmly fastened to any base. "This—ship—of yours gave death to the city. But not only to the city." He paused as if searching for words to make his meaning very clear to her.

"We were a great people—did you not see? We were not then dwellers in ill-made huts! What were we, what might we have been had this not come to us?"

The girl moistened her lips with the point of her tongue. For that she had no answer. It was true that the city she had seen both in her dream and on the screen was something greater than any existing now on this world. Just as, and now she would admit it, in her eyes this Stans was different from the Raski she knew. In him must linger something of the ability which built Kal-Nath-Tan.

"You were a great people," she acknowledged. "A city died, a people were left in shock and despair. But—'' She moistened her lips again. ''What happened after?'' Her own mind began to throw aside the heavy load of sorrow and despair which had clouded her thoughts.

''What happened here was long and long ago. Not in a few years does nature so overlay ruins—or this ship be buried so deeply. Why have your people not found again their stairway upward? They live in their mud huts, they fear all which is different from them, they do not try to be other than they are.''

His frown was black, his lips parted as if he would shout her down, she felt his rage building. Then. . . . The hand which had been deep clenched upon the back of the chair loosened its hold a trifle.

''Why?'' he repeated. She thought he did not ask that of her in return, but rather of himself.

The moment of silence between them stretched even longer this time. His intent stare had shifted from her to the now dead screen behind her shoulders.

''I never thought—'' His voice was lower, the anger in him was yielding. ''Why?'' Now he demanded that of the screen. ''Why did we sink into the mud and remain there? Why do our people bow knee to a King-Head such as Galdor who cares nothing save to fill his belly and reach for a woman? Why?''

Now his eyes came once more to her. There was a fierceness rising in him as if he would have the answers out of her by the force of his will.

''Ask that of the Raski,'' Elossa answered him, ''not the Yurth.''

''Yes, the Yurth!''

She had made a mistake, focusing on her once

again his attention. Still, though there was still anger in him, it was not so great.

"What have you of the Yurth?" He watched her warily as if he expected her at any moment to produce some weapon. "What have you that we hold not? You live in caves and branch huts, no better housed than the rog or the sargon. You wear rough cloth such as cover our laborers in the fields. You have nothing of outward show—nothing! Yet you can walk among us and each and every one, even full of hate, will not raise hand to you. You weave spells. Do you then live among those spells, Yurth?"

"We might. We do not choose to do so. If one deceives himself then he loses everything." Elossa had never really talked to a Raski except on small matters, such as chaffering for food in some market place. What he said, yes, it was a puzzle. She glanced around her at the chamber in which they stood.

This had been made by Yurth, the same Yurth who now lived, as Stans had pointed out, in caves and huts far more primitive than the dwellings of the Raski. Cloth of her own weaving was on her body, and it was coarse and near colorless. She had never really looked upon herself, her people. She had accepted all as part of life. Now, drawing even a little apart, she wondered for the first time. Their life was deliberately austere and grim. Part of the punishment laid upon them?

The same years had passed for Yurth as for Raski. Even as the Raski had not regained what they had lost, so did the Yurth make no move to better the punishment laid upon them. Were both races to live ever so?

"Deceive himself?" Stans broke into her thoughts. "What is deceit, Yurth? Do we inwardly say, we of the Raski, great things were taken from us, so we dare not try to rise to such heights again? Is this our deceit? If so it is time that we face the truth and do not flee from it. And you, Yurth—you who had the stars, because one of your blood made a mistake long ago—are you to walk in penance forever?"

Elossa drew a deep breath. He had challenged her. Perhaps Yurth had gained much with the awakening of the Upper Sense. But, also, perhaps they had accepted that as much of life as they could expect. Now she had a question of her own.

"Have you never asked such questions before, Stans of the House of Philbur?"

He still frowned, but not at her, she guessed. Rather he was seeking some thought he had not tried to capture before.

"I have not, Yurth."

"My name—" Oddly irritated at his form of address, the girl interrupted him, "—is Elossa—we count no Houses in our reckoning."

He looked startled. "I thought—it was always said among us—that the Yurth never spoke their names."

It was her turn to be surprised. What he said was true! She had never known a Yurth to talk so easily to a Raski that names were exchanged. Though the Raski, by custom, were always ready to give their own and that of the First Ancestor of their House. Yet to her now it seemed needful that he stop calling her "Yurth," perhaps because she knew that among his own kind that was a term which was unpleasant.

"They do not," Elossa admitted now, "to those outside the clan."

"But I am not of any clan of yours," he persisted.

"I know." She raised her fingers to press upon her temples. "I am confused. This—this is different."

He nodded. "Yes, Yurth and Raski, by rights we should be in arms against each other. I—I was so earlier. Now I am not." His astonishment was apparent. "In Kal-Nath-Tan there was a horror which entered into me and I did what that made me do. It was not me, and yet a part of me welcomed it. Now I can only wonder at that and see it for a part of the darkness which was, which has always lain there. I ask no forgiveness of you, Elossa." He stumbled a little in pronouncing her name. "For a man who is bred to a task must see it through to the best of his ability. I failed in part, but I do stand where none of my kind have before. I have seen yonder—" He pointed to the screen. "—of the beginning of our hatred, and, also, for the first time seen what I cannot yet understand, the lack in us which keeps us what we are—dirt grubbers who do not dream.

"Are dreams illusions, Elossa? Your kind spin them to aid you. But it seems to me that dreams can in a way serve a man better. He must have something beyond dull thoughts centered on himself and the earth under him to become greater. You Yurth conquered the stars. You are not sky-devils as we think. Now I know that. Rather you are people such as ourselves who had a dream of far voyaging and lived to make it come true.

"Where lies that dream within you now, Elossa? Has it been killed because of your feeling of sin and guilt? What do *you* think beyond yourselves and the ground under you?''

"Little," she answered quietly. "True we seek purpose in all dreams, but we do not use them to change our lives. We are as bound by ancient fears and fates as you. We use our minds to store knowledge but only within narrow limits. To us the Raski are alien. But why?'' She hesitated.

"Why should that be so? In the beginning because you would have been hunted and slain by those maddened by the catastrophe we saw pictured. Later, when your power of mind changed, you—you no longer thought of us any more account than beasts of the woodland. We two speak the truth here and now—is not *that* the truth?

"We were lesser beings, children, to move hither and thither at your bidding when we crossed your path or caught your notice in some fashion. Can you not see that by such an opinion of us you fostered and kept alive the shadow born in Kal-Nath-Tan?''

Elossa accepted the logic of what he said. The bitterness of the city's destruction, the coming of a space-transversing race such as the Yurth destroyed and then replaced with another pattern of thinking. How—how arrogant the Yurth had been—were! They had locked themselves in that arrogance, seeking, they believed, to atone by their own self-exile and austerity. But what they did was sterile, worthless.

Granted that at first they could not live at peace with the Raski, granted that their employment of their machines had altered them irrevocably, yet as time passed they might have sought contacts, turned their talents to the service of the Raski instead of jealously using the Upper Sense for unproductive learning. Their pride of martyrdom was their abiding error. She recognized for the first time Yurth life for what it was, and knew sorrow that it had not been otherwise.

"It is so," Elossa said sadly. "We judged you, and you have been right to judge us. Repentance is necessary, but there are other forms of righting a wrong. In choosing our selfish one we have only compounded the original act many times over. Why have we not seen this?" She ended with rising passion.

"Why have *we* not also seen that we lie in the dust because we have allowed the past to bury us so?" he countered. "We did not need Yurth to build anew. Yet no man reached for the first stone to set as a foundation. We have been locked in our pride also, we of the House of Philbur, looking always to the past and seeking only vengeance for what dashed us from our throne. We have been blind and groping."

"We have been blind and not even groping," she matched him. "Yes, we have talents but we use them only in a little. What might grow here if we harnessed them to a freed will and a living cause?" It was as if she were awaking in this instant from a drugged and drugging sleep in which she had lain all her life, awaking to understand the possibilities which could be ahead. But she was only one. Against her the weight of tradition and custom stood strong, perhaps too stout a wall for her to hope to break.

"Where do we go now, and what do we do?" She was at a loss, seeing this new-found enlightenment as perhaps an even more weighty burden to bear.

"That is a question for both of us," he agreed.

The tenseness had gone out of his body as he fronted her. "The blind do not always welcome sight thrust upon them. They must wish it or they will be frightened. And fear feeds anger and distrust. Between us lies too great a chasm."

"One which can never be bridged?" There was a lost feeling in her. In part this emotion was like that which had come upon her when she witnessed the Yurth farewell to the stars. Were they to be ever imprisoned in the narrow cleft of their misreading or responsibility?

"Only, I think, when Yurth and Raski can speak one with the other face to face, setting aside the past with a whole heart and mind."

"As we have done here?"

Stans nodded. "As we have done here."

"If I," she said slowly, "return to my clan and tell them what has happened, I am not sure I will be heard with any open minds. There are illusions here. We have both dealt with those, suffered from them. Those who made this Pilgrimage before me must have faced the same or their like. Therefore it can be said that I am suffering from a more subtle and deadly illusion. And," she was being honest not only with him but herself now, "I think that that *will* be said. At least by those who have made the Pilgrimage and know the nature of this place."

"If I," he echoed her, "now return to my people and preach cooperation with the Yurth I shall die." His words were blunt but that they were in truth she did not doubt.

"But if I return and do not share what I have learned," Elossa continued, "then I am betraying that part of me which is the deepest and best, for I shall testify to a lie which I might have threatened with the truth. We cannot lie, not and remain Yurth. That is another part of the burden laid upon us by the Upper Sense.''

''And if I return and am killed for speaking the truth—'' He smiled a faint shadow of a smile. ''—then what profit do my people gain? So it would seem we must be liars in spite of ourselves, Lady Elossa. And if it be true that you indeed *cannot* lie, then you face even worse.''

''There are mountains here,'' Elossa said musingly, ''and I can live alone. Yurth blood has this—we are not bred to soft lying or over much food. Who can tell what may lie in the future? Another may come here on the Pilgrimage and see as clearly. A handful of such, from small seed do high-reaching trees eventually grow.''

''You need not be alone. Our own enlightenment is not yet old. Maybe some thinking together upon ways and means can show the two of us how we can do better than stay in perpetual exile. I know that the Yurth choose to dwell apart. Do you still hold to that, also, my lady?''

He was using the address of a high-born Raski to one of equal breeding. She looked at him in wonder as he raised his hand and held it out to her. What he suggested countered every teaching of her life to this minute. But was it not that teaching which had laid hampering bonds upon all her and her blood? Was it not that which must be broken?

''I do not hold to that which would imprison the mind in a false way of thought,'' she replied. She put out her hand slowly, fighting the distaste for flesh meeting alien flesh. There was so much she would have to fight, and to learn, in the future. The time to begin was now.

9

There was a bite in the wind which wailed and moaned around the last vestiges of Kal-Hath-Tan, raised grit of sterile earth to add to the mounding which already half hid the death ship from the sky. Elossa, in spite of her life among stark heights, knowing well the breath of winter there, shivered as she stood at the foot of the walkway which led up into the ancient Yurth ship.

It was not only the chill of that wind which troubled her, there was an inner chill also. She, who had come here to seek out the Secret of Yurth after the custom of her people, had made a hard choice indeed. Learning the manner of the burden which death had laid upon her kind, she had deliberately thereafter chosen not to follow the years-old pattern and return to her clan but rather to try to think in a new way, to hunt a middle road in which Yurth might some day be at peace with Raski and the past be as buried as Kal-Hath-Tan and the ship.

"There is harsh weather to come." Her companion's nostrils quivered as if, like any of the feral dwellers in the heights, he could scent some change in wind which was a warning. "We shall need shelter."

It was difficult for Elossa to believe, even now, that she and a Raski could speak together as if they were of one blood and clan. Most carefully she kept tight rein upon her thought-send, knowing that unless she was ever aware of that, she might unconsciously communicate, or try to, without words. While to the Raski such communication was a dire, abhorred invasion.

She must learn carefully, if not slowly, since they had made this uncertain alliance. Stans claimed to be of a House which had ruled in Kal-Hath-Tan, bred and trained himself for the task of revenge upon the Yurth. But he was also the first of his blood to enter the half-buried ship, and therein learn the truth of what had happened in the very long ago. Learning so, he had deliberately set aside his long-fostered hatred, being intelligent enough to understand that, grievous as the destruction of the city had been through an error of the Yurth space ship, yet upon his people also lay some of the fault. For what had happened since? They had allowed themselves to sink back from the civilization they had once known, choosing to be less than they might be.

Yurth and Raski—Elossa's whole person shrank from any close contact with him, even as he must find in her much which to him was unnatural and perhaps even repulsive.

He did not look at her now, rather he stood gazing out across the mounded ruins of the city toward that distant rise of hills and heights on the other side of the cup-like valley in which Kal-Hath-Tan stood. As tall as she, his darker skin and close-cropped black hair were strange to her eyes. He wore the leather and thick wool of a hunter, and the weapons he carried were those of a roving plainsman.

Accustomed to the standards of the Yurth, Elossa could not truthfully judge, she decided fleetingly, whether he might even be termed fair appearing or not. But his determination, his strength of spirit and resolve, that she accepted as fact.

"There is still time," she said slowly.

As if he, too, had the Yurth power of mind-speech, Stans answered her before she had put her thought entirely into words.

"To forget what we heard and saw, Lady? To go back to those who are willfully blind and who squat in the mud like children who are self-willed and resist all which they should learn? No." He shook his head. "There is no longer any such time for me. Yonder—" With one hand he sketched a gesture to the distant hills. "We can find shelter. And it is best that we strive to do so. Winter comes early in these heights and bad storms strike sometimes with little warning."

Stans did not suggest that they take refuge in the ship, or in that chamber in the mound where he had imprisoned her on her first coming into the ruins. In that choice he was right, Elossa knew. They must both be free of the ancient taint which stained all

which lay here. Only away from the evidences of the
past could they really confront the future.

Thus together they struck out from ruins and ship,
while the star ship's entrance closed behind them,
sealing the secret once more to be ready at the coming of another Yurth seeker. Perhaps a seeker who
might also be persuaded to realize the truth that what
lay in the years behind must not be held about one as
a cloak to deaden in turn the future.

Clouds gathered overhead and the wind grew
stronger, pressing at their backs, as they crossed the
valley, as if it moved to expel them from both ruins
and ship. Stans went warily, continually eyeing the
terrain ahead as if expecting some attack. Elossa
allowed her mind-search to range a little. There was
no life here. But she felt it was best not to bring to
the attention of her companion the results of a gift so
dreaded and hated by all his kind. This, save for
them, was a barren land, left to the long dead.

The pace Stans set was one she could match with
ease, since the Yurth had long since been a roaming
people. He did not speak again, nor had she any
reason to break the brittle silence lying between them.
Their companionship was too new, too untested. And
she had no desire to do that testing.

Twilight was upon them well before they had even
reached the foothills—though those were clear-cut
now, looking as stark and barren as the plain over
which they journeyed. Stans halted at last, pointing
to the left where some stones stood tall as if growing
tree-like from the ground.

''Those can be a windbreak, unless that changes
direction.'' He spoke for the first time since they had

left the ruins. "It is the best shelter we can find hereabouts."

Elossa eyed those stones more doubtfully. She had good reason to believe that they were no natural feature of the earth and plain, rather more ruins. The illusions which might cling to such a place were ever in her mind. Even though such manifestations were only hallucinations to be controlled by Yurth training, still the very vividness with which they could paint themselves on the air could not but stir fear, and fear works upon the stability of the most disciplined mind.

Only Stans was very right, they could not keep on going through the night which was coming so fast. Even a faint promise of shelter away from the wind was to be sought. These are stones only, she told herself. If they hold aught of emotion, an imprint on them strong enough to summon illusions to torment the sensitive, she must armor herself with the truth and dismiss such visions for what they were.

As the Raski had pointed out, they did afford a windbreak. So when the two travelers hunkered down among the rocks they were, for the first time, out of the push of that cold. Elossa opened her journey bag.

Food, drink, both were problems they must face now. The supplies she had carried were scanty and not meant to serve more than one for a few days. She broke one of the coarse meal cakes carefully apart and offered half to Stans. There was water in her bottle, though they must limit themselves to sips until they discovered some river or spring in those heights ahead.

He did not refuse her bounty and he ate slowly as

one mindful that every crumb must be found and munched. Of the water he took very little. When he had done he nodded to the hills ahead.

"The Naxes rises there. Water and game. . . . Also. . . ." Stans paused, frowning, as if his own thoughts had become a puzzle. He rubbed his hand across his forehead and continued, but it was as if he spoke more to himself than to the girl beside him. "There is the cave—the Mouth of Atturn."

"The Mouth of Atturn," she repeated when he again fell silent. "You have knowledge of this place?" The tradition of his House had made him in this generation the guardian of Kal-Hath-Tan. Did he also know more of what lay about the city?

His frown was more intense. "I know," he said with such sharpness as to warn her off any further questioning.

So wrapped in their cloaks they slept behind the stones until Elossa was jerked suddenly out of slumber by some inner warning triggered by the Yurth talent. Over her crouched the Raski hardly visible in the night's darkness. Some trick of the small starlight from overhead touched upon what he held—a bared knife.

Elossa rolled to one side as the knife struck down into the earth where she had lain. But the blow intended to bury steel in her flesh, now slicing into the ground instead, threw Stans off balance. She rolled again, setting between them one of the stones. Getting to her feet now, her staff in hand, the girl waited, her heart beating with force enough to shake her body.

Ruthlessly she reached out with mind-touch. The

wildness of thought she so found was near as upsetting as that attack had been. This was like trapping a mind gone insane. Horror and fear held the Raski in tight grip. And she had a glimpse of a distorted monster. He—he thought that was she!

"Stans!" She cried aloud his name, striving to so awaken him. For it seemed to Elossa that only a man in the hold of a compelling nightmare could be so disoriented.

She heard an answering cry, wild and beast-like. Then she saw him beyond the stones. He was running, on into the darkness of the night. And he went like a man pursued by an unbelievable source of terror.

Shaking, Elossa put out one hand to the stone behind which she had taken refuge. What had happened? All she could guess in answer was that uneasy fear which had been hers earlier—that these stones might generate illusion and one such had worked upon the Raski strongly because of his very heritage.

There was no use in running after him. If the stones were the source of his terror, then once he was out of range, his sanity should again be in control. She opened her mind wide, sent out a questing which lasted only an instant or two since she had no desire to attract any influences which might abide here.

Stans—he was still in flight. She had no desire to try to compel his return. Such an attempt might only heighten his distortion of mind at present.

Once more Elossa settled down in the lee of the stones. To all her cautious probing these remained only rock. It would seem that if they did exude some illusions such were a menace to Raski only.

Though she was uneasy and wanted to stay on guard, she drifted once more into sleep. Then, for a second time, she awoke into dire danger. For she opened her eyes, instantly awake, only to believe for a second or two that she was still caught in some particularly vivid dream.

This was not the plain where she had fallen asleep by the rocks. Instead she stood leaning on her staff in a narrow valley between two rises of hills. There was a season-killed and dry looking brush about. But in the middle of that, directly before her, crouched a sargon, its snarling echoed from the hill walls as a heavy menace.

The beast was a young one, perhaps of this season's litter. But even so immature a sargon was more than a match for any human. While the creature seemed somehow to guess that she must be helpless prey.

Frantically Elossa summoned the authority of mind control. But it was as if her trained thought was over-slow. She could not hold this raving beast nor turn it! She was going to be torn by those claws. She was. . . .

Out of the air came a shrill singing sound. The sargon's flanks quivered as it gathered strength to launch itself upon her. But now it yowled and in its throat showed the shaft end of a crossbow bolt.

Elossa came to life. She unleashed at the creature the full power of her talent. While, at the same time, she flung herself to one side even as she had moved to escape Stans' attack.

The sargon squalled, clawed with one paw at the wound in its throat from which poured a flood of dark blood. Elossa flattened her body tight against the wall of the hill. Between her and the wounded beast there was only a thin growth of brush which the creature could easily break through. But with her thought she prodded as best she could.

As if it had not seen her part-escape moments earlier, the sargon charged forward, breaking down brush. Blood spouted, as its exertions speeded the flow. Again that wailing in the air and a second bolt drove into the body of the frantic beast, placed behind one of its forelegs.

Sprinkling blood widely, the sargon whirled around. Once more it did see her. It was readying for another spring. She could not control this raging alien mind. No one could make a sargon do other than its own will—or. . . .

Perhaps it was the feeling that death was very close to her which speeded Elossa's own thought processes. She dropped her vain attempt to somehow divert the attention of the beast. Instead, with a burst of energy which she rose to only under the lash of fear, she created an illusion. A second Elossa (not too carefully depicted, but at least in the animal's sight enough like its intended prey to draw its attention) now stood before the sargon. The illusion turned and ran. The sargon squalling aloud in its pain and blood lust swung its heavy body around once more to pursue.

It must have so presented the unseen bowman with a better target. For with a third shrilling of flight a bolt found its target. The sargon flung up its head, opened its jaw for a great roar. But it was not sound alone which burst from the beast. Rather a second outpouring of blood fountained down to earth. The

creature took one step and a second, and then toppled. Though it still fought to regain its feet and its
cries sounded strongly, the end had come.

Elossa needed the support of the bank against which
she had taken refuge. That last outpouring of her
talent had weakened her as she had seldom been
since the earliest days of her training. It would take
much rest until she could once more summon even
the lightest of mind-power to her service.

She lifted her head as pebbles and earth cascaded
down the hillside across the narrow valley. Stans half
slid down in their wake. She could not test his mood
by her only defense, not in her present condition.
Though if he meant her harm now he need only have
allowed the sargon to have its way. Or was it that
some touch of the ancient revenge bred in him still
worked to the point that he must take Yurth life by
his own hand?

She stood quietly. In fact she could not have fled,
even if she so wished, all the energy having seeped
out of her. He paused, watching her across the body
of the sargon. Then, without word he knelt to work
his bolts out of the still quivering carcass, deliberately cleansing each in a fashion by driving it point
down into the earth and plucking it forth again.

He no longer looked at Elossa. It was as if she
were invisible. Nor did he speak. What would happen now? Her distrust of the Raski had awakened
once again. Perhaps there was too great a gulf between their two races for any amount of good will to
bridge.

Restoring his bolts to their quiver Stans got to his
feet again. Now he did face her. There was a shade

of expression on his dark face but she could not read it.

"Life for life." He spoke those three words as if they had been forced out of him against his will. What did he mean? That this was in payment of the succor she had given him when he had been clawed by a similar beast on the journey to Kal-Hath-Tan? Or had he saved her now because his attempt in the night had failed and he would be quit of the memory of that? She felt blind when she could not mind-probe for the truth.

"Why," she said at last, "why would you take knife to me? Is your hate from the old days still so strong, Stans of the House of Philbur?"

He opened his mouth as if about to answer and then closed it firmly once more. There was about him an aura of wariness as if he were fronting a possible enemy.

"Why must you take my life, Stans?" she asked again.

He shook his head slowly. "I do not kill," he began and then his head came up proudly and he met her in a fast locking of eyes.

"It was not I. This is a haunted land. It has secrets of things we Raski have long forgotten, which perhaps even you Yurth, with all your dark powers, never knew. There was another will taking over my body. When it did not win what it wished, it left me. I—" Again he frowned. "I think it is different—not Raski as I know, not Yurth. . . . It is very dangerous— perhaps to the both of us."

That this world might have secrets was, indeed, not impossible. Elossa turned her head to look up at the hills about them. They could go back, put into some corner of their minds to be walled there, all that had happened, all they had learned concerning themselves and their people. But she did not believe that was possible. To go on was to venture into the totally unknown. Yet she had a certainty growing within her that this was what could be the only road for her.

"We must go on," Stans said. "There is that—it is like Kal-Hath-Tan—it draws. Or does not that drawing touch you, Lady? I know that you may have no trust in me now, yet in some manner we are bound together."

Elossa tried to summon the talent—to judge— perhaps to feel what he said lay upon him. But she was too exhausted. If she went it would be going blind for a space until her energy was renewed. Resolutely she pushed away from her support.

"I have found water, also the path to the Mouth," he said then. "It is not far."

"Then let us go." So she chose a new road for the second time.

10

So this was the Mouth. Elossa hitched the carry cord of her supply bag up higher on her shoulder, studying the opening before her. Undoubtedly the place had been, or was, some cave opening, natural in these heights to begin with. But there had been the work of man overlaying that of nature. A portion of rock surrounding the opening had been smoothed to provide a surface into which were deep carven, strange mask-like faces.

Or were those separate faces? Rather, it seemed to the girl that they were the same face expressing different emotions, mainly, she decided, malignant ones. Now she asked of her companion, breaking the dividing silence which had lain between them since they had begun the climb to this place:

"You name this 'Mouth of Atturn,' who then—or what then—is Atturn?"

Stans did not glance toward her at all. Instead he

faced the dark opening of the Mouth, into which daylight seemed reluctant to reach, with a faint shadow of fascination on his face. The Raski did not answer at once, as if her words reached him so faintly he scarce heard them at all.

"Atturn?" Now his head did turn slowly, reluctantly. "Atturn—Lady, I do not know. But this was a place of power for the ruling House of Kal-Hath-Tan." He rubbed one hand across his forehead.

"One of your legends? But there must be more," Elossa prodded. Before she entered such a place she wanted to learn all she could. Her experience with Stans in that other underground place beneath the ruins was not such as to encourage her to try a new venture into unknown darkness.

"I—no, I have not heard of this place. But how could that be?" He was plainly not asking those questions of her, rather of himself. "I *knew*, knew the way to this place, that it lay here, that it was shelter. How did I so know that?" That last question was aimed at her this time.

"Sometimes things heard sink into the memory so deeply that only a chance happening calls them forth again. Since the House of Philbur, as you have said, was made protector of the secrets of Kal Hath-Tan it may well be true that this is another scrap of knowledge you ingested without remembering clearly."

"Perhaps." By his expression he was not convinced. "I only know it was necessary for me to come here." He stepped forward as one obeying an order he could not refuse, to pass under the band with its faces on into the Mouth.

But Elossa had one last trial to make. Though her

store of energy had been sadly depleted, still she must draw what she could for this testing. She summoned mindsearch and loosed a probe into the cave. Stans she could pick up instantly, though she made no attempt to contact him—he was merely a registration of consciousness. There were other flickers of lifelight—far down the scale—perhaps insects or other things for whom the Mouth was hunting ground and home. But nothing approaching larger beast or human.

So reassured, she followed on into the dark. For dark it was beyond the small apron of light by the entrance. It was not a cave after all—rather the door to a tunnel.

"Stans!" She paused to call out, having no mind to go blindly on alone. In these heights there must be other caves, ones unused by ancient custom, clean of any man-taint. She knew so little about Raski beliefs. But there was a fact which all Yurth accepted: a place which had been the focus for any emotional experience (and that included temples and ancient dwelling places high on such a list) gathered over the years an aura of force to which those sensitive enough to possess the talent of her people were drawn, maybe even influenced by.

Elossa, remembering that, instantly closed her mind. Until she could be sure no such influences lay here she could only depend upon her body senses. And she felt as one crippled as she hesitated before the dark boring.

"Stans!" she called again.

"Hooooo!" The sound was so echoed and distorted that she could not even be sure the Raski had voiced that call. Then it came again.

"Commmmeee!"

Elossa moved on, cautiously and slowly. She so longed to loose the talent. As her eyes adjusted to the dark she saw very pale bits of radiance along the way. One of those moved and she stopped, startled, stared closer.

A moth or some like winged creature near the size of her own palm was struggling in a web, fighting frenziedly for freedom. It was the lines of that web which gave off the faint light. Then there dropped down toward the fighting prisoner a blackish ball to strike full upon the moth.

Elossa shuddered. Now she could see the other spots of the pale light—more webs spun to catch the unwary. Perhaps their light was the lure to bring their victims closer.

She kept well away from the webbed walls as she went, still slowly. Her staff was now her protection, for she swung that ahead in a slow sweep from side to side to make sure that the way was open. Imagination kept painting for her a picture in which such a web, only a thousand times larger and thicker, might be set across the tunnel itself.

Stans had gone this way, she told herself. Sense did now, however, banish such erratic trails of fear. How had he gotten so far ahead? He must have quickened pace considerably since he had left her company.

Elossa longed to hear his voice, but something kept her from another call. She walked a little faster. Now the lighted webs were missing. Perhaps they only hung where flying things who had blundered in from the outer world could be enticed.

The darkness was very thick. She felt as if she

might reach forth a hand and gather folds of it into her grasp, as one did a shrouding curtain. But the air she breathed was fresh enough and she was aware that there was a small steady current of it now and then touching her cheek.

There came a glow—a sudden leap of red-yellow flames. After the time in the utter dark these seemed nearly as bright as full sunlight and she blinked to protect her eyes against that glare.

Stans stood there, and in his hands was a torch burning bravely. He was thrusting the butt end of that into a stone ring jutting out of the wall as if he knew very well what he was doing. His past denials of such knowledge now made Elossa doubly uneasy.

The torchlight revealed a chamber which must have begun as a cave. But here man's hands had also smoothed and labored to pattern the walls. What the light shone the strongest on was a giant face which covered near the whole of the wall directly ahead. The mouth about a third of the way up from floor level was wide open, a dark cavity into which the light of the torch did not penetrate far.

Eyes as long as Elossa's forearm were pictured wide open. Those did not stare blindly ahead as might those of a statue. Rather they had been fashioned of material which gave them a glitter of life so that she felt that the thing not only saw her but derived some malicious amusement from her presence.

Stans lighted a second torch which he pulled from a tall jar to the left of the face. When he placed that in a twin ring on the opposite side the light was enough to give even more of a knowing look to the stone countenance. The other two walls were bare so that all attention was focused entirely on the leering, jeering face.

Such objects in themselves have little or no natural evil—that comes from without. To say that a carving on the wall was evil was to impute to stone a quality it did not and never had possessed. But to say that an image which had been wrought by those who wished to give evil a gateway into the world was malign was not opposed to that basic truth.

Whoever had carved the face on the wall had been twisted mind and spirit. Elossa had stopped short only a step within the cave room. The illusions which haunted the road to Kal-Hath-Tan had been horrible—born of human suffering to leave the imprint upon the very earth itself. This, this had been cunningly and carefully constructed, not out of great pain of body and shock of spirit, but from a deep desire to embrace all the dark from which man naturally shrinks.

Stans had taken a stand before that face, his arms hanging by his sides, gazing up into those knowing eyes with visible concentration. Almost, Elossa thought, as if he were indeed in communication with whatever power that brutish carving represented.

She kept tight rein upon her talent here, having a feeling that if she loosed even a little—sent out any probe—what might answer would be. . . .

Elossa shook her head. No! She must not allow her imagination to suggest terrors which could not exist. That this may have been a ''god,'' the focus for some horrible and evil religion, and so have drawn to it the energy sent forth by the worshipers, perhaps even the terror of sacrifices, that was the truth. But in itself it was nothing but cleverly fashioned stone.

"Is this Atturn?" She felt the need to break the silence, to shake Stans out of that concentration. He did not answer. She dared to go forward, and, putting aside the distaste of the Yurth for body contact, she laid her hand upon his arm.

"Is this then Atturn?" she repeated in a louder voice.

"What?" Though Stans turned his head to look at her Elossa felt he did not really see her at all, that his gaze did not meet hers but in some manner still set upon the face.

Then there was a flicker of change in his expression. That deep concentration broke. That he came alive again was the only way she could explain the change in him to herself.

"What?" He swung away from her to look once more at the face, so well lighted by the torches he had set. "What? Where? Why?"

"I asked . . . is this. . . ." Elossa gestured to the face. "Atturn. He . . . it . . . seems certainly to have a mouth."

Stan's hands covered his eyes. "I—I do not know. I cannot remember."

Elossa drew a deep breath. Last night this Raski had tried to kill her as she slept. In the light of morning, after she in turn had been possessed (for what other than possession had sent her sleepwalking then into the path of the sargon) he had saved her life. He had brought them here, plunging through the darkness of the tunnel as if he knew what lay at its end, lighted the torches with the surety of one who knew exactly where to find the waiting brands and the strike stone.

"You know this place well indeed," Elossa continued, determined to pin the Raski to some admission. "How else could you have found those?" She pointed to the torches. "A hidden temple for your ancient vengeance to which you have brought me for slaying."

She did not know why she chose to make that accusation; it was out of her mouth almost before she realized what she said. But the possible truth of it alerted her to a danger which might also be real.

"No!" He threw out his hands as if he were repulsing that gap-mouthed face, repudiating all that it might mean. "I do not know, I tell you!" His voice was heating with anger. "It is not me . . . it . . . is something else which makes me its servant. And . . . I . . . will . . . not . . . serve . . . it!" He said that last sentence slowly and with emphasis upon every word as heavy as a blow he might seek to deliver against an enemy's body. That he believed in what he said now Elossa did not doubt. But that he could summon any defense against the compulsion which had twice ruled him, of that she had no surety at all.

The Raski swung around, his back to the face. There was a demand for belief in his expression. His mouth firmed into a thin line of determination, his jaw squarely set.

"Since I cannot control this—this thing which moves me to its will—then it is better that we part. I should walk alone until I can be sure that I am not just a tool."

That made good sense—except for one thing. The night before she had in turn been moved unknowing, walking in her sleep, straight toward death. Yet her race had bred into them, or she always so believed, mental barriers against any such tampering. No Yurth could master the mind of one of his fellows, nor could he control even a Raski, who had no such safeguards, for more than the building of short-lived hallucinations.

This was not a matter of hallucinations, it dealt with mental power of sorts on a level totally foreign to Elossa. And that aroused a sickly dread within her. Yurth talent had always seemed supreme, perhaps they had grown unconsciously arrogant in what they knew and could do. Perhaps even, her mind produced a very fleeting thought, it was the burden of the old sin which hovered ever over them as a true necessity to preserve their code of what the talent might and might not be used for.

Was it because she had shrugged aside Yurth Burden that she had somehow also fallen under the command of this unknown factor which Stans recognized and which she must believe had some existence? If that were her fault, then it was true she, as much as the Raski, had assumed a new burden—or curse—and must learn either to dispel or bear it.

"It moves me also," she said. "Did I not nearly walk into the jaws of a sargon without being aware of what I did?"

"This is not Yurth." He shook his head. "It is somehow of Raski—of this world. But I swear to you, on the Blood and Honor of my House, I know nothing of even any legend of this place, nor how I have been led to where it lies, nor why I am here. I do not worship devils, and this is a thing of evil. You can smell its stench in the air. I do not know Atturn, if this *is* Atturn.''

Again she must accept that he spoke what was to him the utter and complete truth. Raski civilization had ended once in the great trauma of the destruction of Kal-Hath-Tan, the which she had witnessed herself in a vision. Though the people lived on, some inner spring of their courage, pride, and ambition had been broken. Much which must have been known in the days before the Yurth ship had blasted their city certainly was now lost.

Yet they stood now in a center of power. She could detect its force, like small fingers sliding over the shield she kept upon her mind, as if something curious and very confident strove to find an answer to the puzzle she presented. The farther they could get from this place, the better.

Elossa swayed. Through that mental shield, seemingly through her body, too, with a flash of pain as might follow a stroke of enemy steel had come that cry, Yurth! Somewhere—not too far away—one of Yurth blood was in danger, had loosed the call which was the ultimate in pleas, that was used only when death itself must be faced.

. Without thinking she instantly dropped her barrier, sent forth her own questing search call. Once more came the other, lower, far less potent.

Which way? She had swung around to face the tunnel opening. Outside—which way? She sent an imperative demand for the unknown to guide her.

For the third time the call sounded. But not from the direction she was facing at all. No, behind her. Elossa pivoted to front the face. The seeing eyes glittered with malice. That call had come from behind—from out of the face! Yurth blood spilt here in some ancient sacrifice, leaving a strong residue of emotion which another Yurth could tap? No, it was too vivid in that first summons. Surely she would have sensed the difference between a reminder of the dead and a plea formed by the yet living. There was a Yurth in peril here somewhere—behind the wall and the evil, open mouth of Atturn.

11

Now it was Stans' hand which caught at her.

"What is it?"

"Yurth," Elossa answered distractedly, so concentrated on trying to trace that cry that she did not even try to free herself from his unwelcome touch. "Somewhere there is Yurth blood in trouble. Somewhere—there!"

The girl went to her knees before that open mouth in the wall. Recklessly she aimed a thought-probe.

Yurth! Yes, but—something else also . . . alien. . . . Raski? She could not be sure. She forced herself forward and lifted the staff, pointing one end of it into the mouth as if it were a weapon both to attack that which might lie waiting in the shadowed pit of the opening, or defend herself against that which might issue forth.

The shaft slipped in and in. That opening was no shallow one. It was as if it were a second entrance leading perhaps to another way through a maze of threaded caves. She must know. . . .

Elossa closed her eyes, drew steadily upon what energy had returned to her. Yurth—where waited Yurth?

Her thought touched nothing, no mind. Still she was very sure there had been no mistaking that first cry. Where then?

A sound shattered her concentration. Startled, she glanced up from where she crouched with nearly all of her staff fed into the open mouth. Stans swayed, his hands clawed at the breast of his jerkin as if those fingers would forcibly strip the clothing from him, while his face was such a mask of mingled fury and fear that Elossa started back, jerking the staff free of the mouth to hold ready in her own defense.

As he weaved from side to side she gained a strange impression that he was fighting, fighting something she could not see, perhaps something which lay within himself. A small fleck of foam appeared at one corner of his twisting lips. He gasped, hoarse sounds at first, then words:

"Kill—it would have me kill! Death to the sky-devils! Death!"

Now it was he who went to his knees. As if he could not control them, his hands shot toward her, fingers crooked, reaching for her throat.

"No!" That cry was close to a scream. With a visible and terrible effort he swung his body half around, brought both fists down on the upper lip of the stone mouth. There was a crack opening in that stone, blood on his knuckles. The stuff of the face crumbled as if it were no more than sun-dried clay. It sloughed away, not only that protruding portion of the lip where the full force of his blow had fallen but more and more—cracks running up and down—away from that point of contact. Shards of what had seemed solid rock cascaded down into rubble on the floor.

Even those eyes shattered with a high tinkling sound as might come from the cracking of glass. Those, too, sloughed away, fell to become a powder-glitter. The face was gone. Only a hole framing darkness, into which no bit of the torchlight appeared to enter, marked now the mouth of that god—or devil, or whatever the face on the wall had been intended to portray.

But with the crumbling of the mask there was a change in the chamber. Elossa straightened, feeling as if she had just loosened, to drop from her shoulders some burden she had not been aware until that moment she carried. What was gone was the presence of evil, vanished with the destruction of the face.

Stans, still on his knees before the hole, shivered. But now his head came up and the conflict which had distorted his face was gone. There passed a shadow of bewilderment across his features and then came purpose.

"It would have made me kill," he said in a low voice. "It would drink blood."

Elossa stooped and picked up a bit of the rubble. It seemed strange that Stans' single blow had brought about such complete destruction. Between her fingers this bit had the solidity of stone. Though she applied pressure she could not crush it further.

She might not understand what had happened, but

what must be done now was plain. If she were to answer that plea from Yurth to Yurth, she must enter what had been the Mouth of Atturn. Though every instinct in her arose in revulsion against the act.

"You did not kill." The girl once more picked up her staff. "Therefore it did not rule you, even though it tried." She had no idea what that "it" might be. In this place she was ready to accept belief in some force, immaterial perhaps, wedded to the face. Why Stans' blow had been enough to send it into oblivion (if he had, the chance might well be that this freedom was only a temporary thing) she might not understand. But she must accept a fact she had witnessed.

He stared straight at her. His frown was one of doubt.

"This I do not understand. But I am myself, Stans of the House of Philbur! I do not answer to the will of shadows—evil shadows!" There was both pride and defiance in that.

"Well enough," she was willing to agree, "but there lies the road for our taking now."

Elossa had not the slightest wish to crawl into the mouth. Only that age-old compulsion laid upon her race—that no cry for help sent mind to mind could be disregarded—was such that she could not deny it.

It was Stans who wrested one of the torches from its holder and who then, with that in hand, got down to crawl through the mouth. Elossa hesitated only long enough to seize upon another of the unlit brands stacked in the corner of the cave. With that, and her staff under one arm, she followed.

The light of the torch was dimmer somehow than it had been in the cave room, while the passage remained both low and narrow, to be negotiated only on hands and knees. Stans' body half blotted out the light ahead, but there was very little to see, save that the walls of this rounded way were smoothed and the flooring under them, though stone, was also free of even dust or grit.

Elossa had to struggle against a rising uneasiness. This was not be recognized, as she had the atmosphere in the cave room, as from any real cause. It was rather that she was aware that over and around her was solid stone, the weight of which was a threat. The memory of how that which had appeared firm in the form of the face had so easily shattered under Stans' single blow was ever in her mind. What if an unlucky brush against ceiling or side wall brought about such a collapse here, to bury them without hope or warning?

Then she saw Stans' dark body disappear. But the light he had carried, after a swing out of sight, swiftly dropped again to guide her from that worm's path into again a larger space.

There had been no attempt here to trim walls or smooth flooring. This was a cave nature had wrought. A drift of sand and gravel lay at her feet as the girl stood up beside the Raski. Perhaps one time water had washed its way through here as some earth-hidden stream.

Stans swung the torch back and forth. Its light did not reach to any roof over their heads: they might well be standing at the bottom of a deep chasm, while the side walls showed faults and breaks in plenty. There was no indication which of those might mark an exit.

Once more Elossa shut her eyes and centered her talent upon a seeking-thought. No answer. Yet she was sure that that Yurth cry had not been followed by death. That ending would have reached her as a shock since she had held her mind open to pick up the smallest hint of response.

Stans moved slowly along the walls, deliberately shining his torch into each fissure he passed. But Elossa had sighted something else. The drifted sand on the floor did not lay smooth and unmarked in all places. Though it might be too soft to hold any recognizable print yet she was sure that what she sighted well to the left were traces left by the feet of some traveler.

"There." She indicated them to the Raski. "Where do those lead?"

He held the torch closer, then followed the scuffed marks. Those headed directly to another fissure, seemingly no different from the rest.

"This is deeper," he reported, "well able to be a way on—or out."

At least this time they did not have to go on hands and knees, though the way was a very narrow one and in places they had to turn sidewise to struggle through, the rough rock scraping their bodies. Nor did the path run straight as the two others they had followed.

Sometimes they had to scramble up a steep rise, climbing as if the way were a chimney. Again there came a sharply right-angled turn left or right. Then a last effort issued them into a second rough cave.

The torch was sputtering near its end. Elossa was well aware that they had been traveling a long time.

She was hungry and, though they had taken sips of
water from their journey bottles (filled to the brim at
the stream Stans had found before they entered the
mouth) there was a dryness which seemed to come
from the very air of this maze to plague their mouths
and throats.

This new cave was small and what they faced
along one side was a wall, plainly built by purpose to
be a barrier. The stones which formed it were not
laced together by mortar. But they had been wedged
and forced solidly into a forbidding mass.

Stans worked the butt of the torch into a niche at
one end of that wall, then ran his hands along its
rough surface.

"It is tight enough," he commented. "But. . . ."
He drew his long-bladed hunting knife to pick carefully with the point at a crevice between two rocks
near his shoulder level. "Ahhh. . . ." Holding the
knife between his teeth, he wriggled the larger of the
two stones back and forth and then gave a sudden
jerk which brought it out of its setting.

With that gone two more rattled down and Stans
kicked them back toward the way they had come. "It
looks stronger than it is," he announced. "We can
clear this without trouble, I think."

The space was cramped so that only one might
pick at the wall at a time. They took turns at that
labor, passing the freed chunks to the other to be
cleared away. Elossa's arms and back began to ache.
She was as hungry as one at the mid-winter fasting.
But at present she had no wish to suggest that they
pause either to rest or to share the fast dwindling

supplies she carried. To be out of this underground
hole was far more important.

When they had cleared a space large enough to
squeeze through Stans collected the torch once again.
He thrust that ahead of him into the aperture and a
moment later Elossa heard him give a surprised
exclamation.

"What is it?" she demanded trying to edge closer.

He did not answer; instead he forced his way
beyond and she was as quick to follow. Again they
passed from cave to man-made way. Not only were
the walls of this new and wide passage smooth, but
they also appeared to have been coated with a substance which gave off the sheen of polished metal.
The torchlight brought color to blaze also—ribbons
and threads of it wove long, curling strips on the
smooth surface. Gem bright those appeared—scarlet,
deep crimson, flaunting yellow, rust brown, a green
as vividly alive as the new leaves of spring, a blue
as delicate as the shading on the snows of the
mountains.

There was no design in it Elossa could see, just a
rippling of long lines and bands. Nor did the color of
any one of those remain the same—yellow became
green, blue deepened to red.

At first she had welcomed this change, finding in it a
certain relief after the drab gray of the rock. Then she
blinked. Was there something alien about those bands,
threatening? How could color threaten?

She remembered the colored towers, palaces, walls
of Kal-Hath-Tan as it had stood in her vision
before death descended upon it. The city had appeared a giant chest of jewels spilled idly across the

land. Just as bright as these bands. But there was a difference.

Stans swept the torch closely along the wall fronting them. The bank he chose so to illumine began green, became abruptly scarlet, continued orange, then yellow. He reached out and tapped a nail against that colorful ribbon and Elossa, in the silence of this passage, heard the faint answering click-click.

"This is of Kal-Hath-Tan?" she asked. She shielded her eyes a little with her hand. It appeared, she thought now, that the colors held the torch-light, brightened it. It certainly could not be only her imagination that her eyes smarted as if she had gazed too long into some source of light far stronger than the torch.

"I do not know. It is unlike anything I have ever seen. It—it seems as if it should have a meaning of importance, and yet it does not. Only there is the feeling. . . ."

She did not know how sensitive one of his race might be to influences designed by his own kind. But that this place made her more and more uncomfortable could not be denied. The sooner she—they—found a way out the better.

"Which way do we go?"

Stans shrugged. "It seems to be a matter for guessing."

"Right, then." Elossa said quickly, since he made no move to do any of that guessing.

"Right it will be." Almost like a fighting man on parade he gave a half turn and started right.

The passage was much wider, they could walk abreast without any difficulty. But they went on in silence. Elossa took more and more care to keep her eyes strictly ahead, trying not to glance at the bands of color. There was a pull there, like the beginning of some illusion.

Also, the farther they went, the wider the bands became. Those which had been the width of a finger at the point where they had broken into the passage were now palm size. Others could span her arm, shoulder to wrist.

The colors could not glow any brighter, but their change from one hue to another was far more abrupt, creating a dazzlement which reacted more and more on her sight. She walked now with hands cupping eyes to cut out the side view.

Perhaps it was affecting Stans also, though he said nothing, for he was quickening pace, until they moved at a steady trot. As yet they had discovered no break in the walls, and in the shadow beyond the reach of the torch the way seemed to continue endlessly.

Elossa uttered a small cry, staggered toward the wall on her right.

Yurth call—so loud and clear that he or she who had uttered that cry might be standing just before them. Only there was no one there.

"What is it?" Stans' hoarse voice held a note of impatience.

"Yurth—somewhere close. Yurth and danger!"

Now that she was so certain that they must be very close to that which had drawn her here, Elossa called, not with the mind-send this time but uttering one of the carrying summons which her people used in their mountain faring, each clan having its own particular signal.

There was movement in the shadows which lay ahead. Stans held the torch higher, took a step or so forward to see the better.

A figure, yes. Human in that it stood erect and came walking toward them. Elossa's hand arose in the greeting between Yurth and Yurth.

12

Yurth in feature the stranger certainly was. But his clothing was different. In place of the leggings, the coarse smock, the journey cloak, all of drab coloring which made up the uniform body covering of her kind, this newcomer's slender form was covered with a tight-fitting suit which left only the hands and the head from the throat up bare. It was of a dark shade which could have been either a near black-green or blue, and so fitted to the flesh and muscles it covered that it seemed another skin.

She had seen such before.

Elossa's hands tightened on her staff. Yes! This she had seen before, both in the pictures painted by the hallucinations guarding Kal-Hath-Tan and in those she had witnessed in the sky ship when she had learned the true meaning of the Yurth Burden. This Yurth wore the dress of the ship people—as if he had not been here generations but had this very hour stepped from his space voyaging ship, now half buried in the earth which was Raski world.

"Greeting . . . brother. . . ." She used the speech of her people, not the common tongue which they shared with Raski.

But there was no lightening of expression on that other's face, no sign that he knew her as one of common heritage with himself. Rather there was a glitter in his wide-open eyes, a set to his mouth, which awoke in her the beginnings of uneasiness. She tried the mind-speech. There was—nothing! Not a barrier, just nothing she could touch. Her amazement was so great that she was frozen for a second or two, while the hand of the Yurth moved, bringing into line with her breast a rod of black which he held.

"No!" Stans crashed against her, the weight of his body bringing them both down on the hard stone under their feet with a bruising force. Across where she had stood moments earlier there swept a beam of dazzling light. Heat crackled through the air so that, even though Elossa lay well below where the beam had sped, still she felt the touch of its fire through her thick clothing.

It was not the shock of the attack which had rendered her helpless for the moment, rather the understanding that nothing, no one, had fronted her. By the evidence of the mind-send there had never been any Yurth there at all! But the weapon? That had been no part of any hallucination—surely it could not!

She gathered her wits, struggled against the hold that Stans had on her. There was no Yurth—there could not be! She pulled around to find she was right. The passage was empty. But—on the floor—only a little beyond where she lay now with Stans' weight still half over her, was the tube weapon the stranger had carried.

"He . . . it . . . is gone!" Stans loosed her and arose to his feet. "What . . ."

"Hallucination." she said. "A guardian. . . ."

Stans bent over the tube but did not touch it. "He was armed—he shot fire with this. Can a hallucination do such things?"

"Such can kill, yes, if he or she who sees them believes that they are real."

"And they carry such weapons—real weapons?" Stans persisted.

Elossa shook her head. "I do not know. It is not known to my people that they can do so." She eyed the tube. It had not vanished with its owner, or user, but still lay there, concrete evidence that they *had* been fired upon.

To take that up would equip her with a weapon far better than any defense she had ever had. But at the same time she could not bring herself to touch it. She got to her feet, leaning on her staff for support. Stans reached for the tube.

"No!" she cried sharply. "We do not understand the nature of that. Perhaps it is not of our world at all."

Stans sat back on his heels and looked up at her, frowning a little.

"I do not understand this talk of hallucinations. Nor can I believe in a man who stands there, fires death at us, and then vanishes, leaving his weapon behind. How does Yurth come into the Mouth of

Atturn, and what does he here, besides striving to put an end to us?''

Again Elossa shook her head. ''I have no answer for you. Save that it is best not to take to yourself anything such as that.'' With her staff she pointed to the tube. ''And. . . .''

But she just caught sight of something amid that banding on the wall. There was a difference in the texture there—yes! And directly across from it, on the opposite side, another such spot. She reached out with her staff and, not quite touching the wood to the wall itself, outlined a square on either side about breast high and the size of her two palms flattened out together.

''Look!''

Stans slewed around at her command, gazing from one side of the corridor to the other.

''Did not the Yurth stand between these two?'' the girl demanded.

His frown deepened. ''I think so. But what of it?''

''Perhaps not a hallucination.'' She was trying hard to remember fragments of old stories from her people. Though they had never spoken of Kal-Hath-Tan and the Burden of Yurth to those who had not made the Pilgrimage which set upon them the seal of responsibility and maturity, yet they had tales of long ago. She had always known that there was little in common between her people and the world on which they were uneasy prisoners. They had had a far more glorious past than they dared hope to achieve ever again.

On the buried sky ship she had learned just how adept the Yurth had been in strange powers. It could be that what they had seen here had not indeed been a hallucination after all, but a real Yurth transported by some means now beyond her comprehension to defend a hiding place against Raski invasion—transported by mechanical means and now returned to his hiding place.

If the Yurth in such concealment had had no contact with the rest of their people then to such a one she would seem a Raski even as was Stans, thus an enemy. How could she communicate with these hidden Yurth?

But, why had the mind-touch registered as if there had been no one there? Could she begin to imagine what powers these ship people had had in their time—the knowledge they had put aside when they had taken up the heavy burden of what they believed to be their great sin against this world?

"If it were not a hallucination," Stans broke into her absorbed whirl of thought, "then what did we see? A spirit of the dead? Do spirits then carry weapons which they can use? We might have been cooked by that fire!"

"I don't know!" Elossa snapped, out of her own ignorance and awaking anger. "I do not understand. Save there are plates on the wall here and here." Once more she indicated those with her staff. "And he whom we saw stood between them." Now she dared to use her staff to probe at the rod on the floor, turning it over. Even in the limited light from the bands on the wall they could both see now that, though it had thrown a lethal beam at them, it could never do so again. The under side of the cylinder so exposed showed a hole melted, as if some great heat had eaten away the metal.

"It must have been very old," Stans drew the first conclusion from that evidence. "Too old to use—as old as the sky ship."

"Perhaps." But the useless weapon was not the important thing. *That* was the appearance of the Yurth, and that cry for help which had brought her here. She had not been mistaken in that. Somewhere Yurth still had being and were in danger.

"You must know more," she rounded on Stans, "of your own history seeing those of your House were pledged to watch Kal-Hath-Tan, to seek out Yurth who came and demand satisfaction from them for your city's death. Where we stand you say is the Mouth of Atturn. Who *is* or was Atturn? What had Yurth to do with such a place? If this was a temple. . . ." She drew a deep breath, remembering now some of the things which had flitted ghost-like through the mounds of Kal-Hath-Tan—the hunting to horrible deaths of the ship's people who had tried to render aid to the city they had destroyed by chance. Had Yurth been dragged here, to be sacrificed in torment to some Raski god or force? Was *that* the plea, sent thundering down the years by dying men and women, which indeed lingered now to entrap her also?

"Was Yurth blood shed here?" She ended her demand harshly.

Stans had risen once more to his feet, though he kept a careful distance, she noted, from the two plates in the walls apparently having no desire to pass between those.

"I do not know," he answered quietly. "It may well be so. Those of Kal-Hath-Tan were maddened, and they carried into madness their hatred. I cannot remember anything of Atturn nor why I was drawn to the Mouth. In that I speak the full truth. Enter into my mind if you wish, Yurth, and you will see that is so."

He called her "Yurth," she noted; perhaps their precarious partnership might not long survive. But she did not need to obey his suggestion and mind-probe. It was an offer he would not have made if he had anything to hide. The Raski hated too much the powers they believed Yurth used ever to speak as he had except in complete truth.

The corridor still stretched ahead. To retreat might be the way of safety. Only with the Yurth call still in her mind Elossa could not take the first step back. Too long had those of her blood been conditioned to support each other, to answer to such a plea with all the help they might give.

"I must go on." She said that to herself rather than to the Raski. But now she added to him, "This is no call that you are in honor pledged to answer. You saved me from flame death which some manifestation of my own people turned upon me. If you are wise, Stans of the House of Philbur, you will agree that this is no quest of yours."

"Not so!" he interrupted. "I can no more turn from this path than can you. What drew me to the Mouth still works in me."

He was silent for a breath or two, and when he spoke again there was the heat of anger in his voice. "I am caught in something which is not of my time. I know not what power holds me but I am surely as captive as if I wore the chains of an overlord on my wrists!"

He was eyeing her with the suspicion and rage which had been a part of him when they had fronted each other in the sky ship. The fragile meeting of minds which they had carried from that encounter might be entirely broken, Elossa decided unhappily. To face the unknown with a potential enemy by one's side was to compound all peril lying in future. Yet surely they *were* tied together in some strange fashion.

"It would be best," she suggested, "not to pass directly between those." Once more she indicated the plates on the wall. Crouching, she obeyed her own warning by going on hands and knees under the setting of the squares. Without hesitation the Raski followed her example.

They went more warily, Elossa herself now keeping a keen eye on the walls, glancing ever from one side to the other, in search of more such insets as that which had marked the coming of the Yurth in ship's clothing. She retained a close rein on her mind, blanketing down as best she could all emanations which another might pick up if some wide-flung mind-search were in progress.

According to the message left in the sky ship the development of Yurth talent had been a latter thing with her people, a deliberately fostered attribute which the ship's equipment had set upon them after the great catastrophe. Perhaps some of the Yurth who could might have fled before that plan had been enacted, might have escaped similar development. Yet the call had been on mental level only.

Even if there had been a body of survivors from the ship come into hiding here in the heart of these mountains, how many generations were they away from the first of the refugees? The man she had seen wearing the ship's clothing—clothing which looked untouched by time. . . .No, he *must* have been an illusion.

They went warily, at a pace which gave them a chance to survey carefully the passage ahead. That continued to run straight, the color lines on its walls, growing wider until their edges met and there was no neutral background to be seen. Elossa felt an ache develop behind her eyes; to survey those colors as she thought it needful to do hurt so that her eyes teared and smarted.

In a queer fashion the colors themselves made her feel ill and she slowed yet more, finding it necessary to pause now and then, closing her eyes to rest them. Stans had said nothing since they had started on, but suddenly he broke the silence between them:

"There is—"

He had said no more than those two words when, in the air, suspended, without a visible support, there appeared a mist which whirled about, gathering substance as it moved. From a small core it grew larger until it filled the full passage from the rock under their feet to that which roofed them overhead, spreading in turn from one side wall to another.

As it solidified it became the same monstrous mask which had surrounded the mouth hole giving passage into this underground territory. The eyes of the mist face held the same malicious glitter—even, Elossa thought, more awareness than those set in the rock. Once more the mouth was agape as if providing a door to some threatening way beyond. Though through it she could see no spread of the corridor, only deep darkness.

"Atturn!" Stans gave the manifestation a name. "The Mouth—it waits to swallow us!"

"Illusion!" The girl countered with a firmness she could not altogether feel.

There was a stir within the open cavern of that mouth. Though the rest of the face was now appearing very solid, the mist which it formed no longer moved as far as she could see. Out of the opening there licked a tentacle of darkness, as if some great black tongue quested for them.

Elossa, without thinking, reacted on the physical level, stabbing at that with her staff. Then she realized her mistake. One did not fight such as this with force of arm—rather force of mind. But before she could ready such counter the staff had passed through the tongue without any visible effect. And that lash of darkness closed about Stans, closed tightly and clung. In spite of his efforts to free himself, the Raski was drawn forward to where the lips quivered, awaiting him. There was an avid excitement in the eyes of that face, a kind of terrible greediness to be read about the waiting mouth. Atturn would feed and this food was now within its power.

Elossa caught at Stans, taking firm hold of his shoulder. There was no disguising the pull which drew him with a strength which they could not match, even linked in common struggle. But the girl needed that contact in order to apply her own answer.

"You are not!" She cried aloud in her mind to that face. "You have no being here and now! You are not!" She launched her arrows of denial even as she would have sent ones of wood, metal-tipped, from a hunting bow. If only Stans could help her! This manifestation must be of Raski, even as the other had been of Yurth.

"It is not there!" she cried aloud. "This is a thing of illusion only. Think of it so, Stans! You must deny it!" She returned to her own fierce denial by force of mind.

The strength of the tongue appeared limitless. Stans was nearly at the verge of those lips opened even wider to engulf him, while Elossa had been drawn also through the hold she kept on the Raski.

"You are not!" Now she both cried that aloud and thought it with all the force she could summon.

Was it only her imagination, or did the awareness in those great eyes flicker?

"You are not!" She had not said that. It was Stans who had uttered that breathless, low cry. He had stopped fighting against the loop of darkness about his body, instead, with upheld head and defiant gaze he faced the eyes boring down at him.

"You are not!" he repeated.

There was no general loosing of his bonds. Instead the face, the tongue which held him, the whole of the illusion vanished in an instant between one breath and another, so quickly that they both stumbled forward, carried by the very impetus of their resistance when the source against which they fought disappeared.

13

Not only had the face which barred their passage vanished, but so had the passage itself. Those smooth walls with the bands of color winked out. In their place was a sweep of dark on either side. The torch which they had forgotten when they had worked their way through into the band-lighted passage was no longer alight to give them any idea of the extent of this pocket of deep dark.

Elossa stood very still, shivering. She had the impression that they were no longer in any confined corridor. Rather there must stretch about them, for some distance, an area which might hold deadly snares for any who blundered on. The fear of the dark unknown which was bred into her kind sought now to send her into panic, and she needed all the resources of spirit she could muster to remain self-disciplined, turn in upon what senses of hearing and smell she might draw upon, since sight was denied her.

"Elossa." For the first time her companion spoke her name. She was startled in that his voice seemed to come from some distance away. Yet, though that one word echoed hollowly, there was no trace of fear in it. ·

"I am here," she returned, schooling her own voice as best she could to the same level. "It remains— where are *we*?"

She nearly cried out as, from the smothering darkness, a hand fell on her shoulder, slipped down her arm, until fingers found and tightened about her wrist.

"Wait. I have still the fire-strike." Those fingers which had gripped her, perhaps in mutual reassurance for an instant, loosed hold.

She heard the click-click of what could only be a striker in use. There followed a small flare of flame. That grew and she saw, with a thankfulness she did not try to put into words, that Stans had not abandoned his torch, though she had not remembered now seeing it in his hands as they passed along the corridor.

Such a small light hardly pressed back any of the dark. Still it illumined their two faces, and, in a way, built up a measure of defense against the pressing blackness. Stans held it between them for a long moment as if so to reassure them both that they did indeed have it. Then he swung it away, out before them, nearly at shoulder level.

The flames flickered, leaped and fell. Elossa could feel against her own cheek currents of air which puffed, flowed, then were gone again. But the light did not touch any wall, on either side, before, or behind. They might have been dropped on a wide open, lightless plain. Under foot was a solid surface of dark rock, the only stable thing they had yet sighted. Had the corridor been entirely illusion? Elossa, for all her awareness of how the conscious mind might be manipulated and tricked, could hardly accept that. If it had not been illusion in entirety then how had they been transported into this pocket of eternal night?

"There is a current of air. See, the torch," Stans said. "Our best guide may lie with that."

It was true that the flames were blown away from the head of the brand he held. His suggestion was undoubtedly the most sensible one. They turned to face that current, the flames pointing toward their own breasts.

But they kept their pace slow. Now and then Stans paused, holding the torch out to this side or that. There was still no walls to be seen. Finally the light shone out on the lip of a drop. There the Raski lay belly down, to crawl cautiously to the edge of that, holding the torch out and down. There was nothing to see below but a chasm apparently so deep that their light was quickly lost in it.

Yet it was from across this that the current of air blew. Stans sat up. The small part of his face Elossa could glimpse by the weaving flame was set. However, she saw no suggestion of wavering or weakness in his frowning gaze as he turned his head slowly from left to right surveying the rim of the drop on which they crouched.

"With a rope," he said as if more than half to himself, "we might try descent. We cannot otherwise."

"Along the edge then?" Elossa was privately very

dubious that they would find any way of bridging that gulf. On the other hand there just might be a faint chance that the break itself would eventually narrow so that a leap could take them over.

He shrugged. "Right or left?"

It was all a matter of chance. One way might be as good as the other. During the moments of rest here she had been sending out short mind-probes, striving to find even the most minute suggestion of other life here—life which might have its own paths and ways to reach again the surface of the world she knew. The puzzle of the Yurth cry for help still troubled her mind.

"It matters not to me." She returned from the emptiness in which her probe had been lost and useless.

"Left then." The Raski got to his feet. He waited until she, too, stood up, and then turned in the direction he had chosen, keeping near enough to the edge of the drop so the rim lay ever within the light of the torch.

There was little way to measure distance traveled, save in the fatigue of their own bodies. Elossa found herself counting steps under her breath for no good reason, save that such a sum of their journey quieted the ever-present fear that there was no way out.

Then—

Stans gave a sharp exclamation, strode forward. The light of the torch had caught a projection out from the rim of the chasm, extending over the dark emptiness of that drop. It was of the same rock as formed the flooring over which they had traveled, and narrowed as it went. Not worked stone of any man-made bridge, Elossa thought. Yet. . . .

Her companion swung the torch closer to the surface of that projecting tongue. Though there were no marks of tools smoothing this path there lay something else. Deep carven into the floor was another representation of that face, while extending from it was the bridge in the form of a tongue thrust forth. Elossa halted just beyond the edges of the carving, having no wish to tread over the wide lips of the mouth. But Stans apparently felt no such repugnance. He stepped onto the tongue where it issued from between the lips at its widest extent. Then he knelt and, torch in one hand, began to crawl out on the bridge itself, if bridge it was.

Elossa had no desire to follow. There was that about this continual appearance of Atturn's face which disturbed her. It was wholly of Raski, and yet Stans insisted that he knew little of it. There was also the fact that whoever had wrought the representations of it she had seen had continually accented the malice, the evil. Atturn had not been a god—or ruler—or energy—who had been engaged in any good for her own kind.

She watched Stans creep along over the drop, longing to summon him back. Yet she knew better than to disturb the concentration displayed in his whole tense figure. While the tongue bridge, though it narrowed, did seem solid enough as far as the torchlight reached.

Stans paused, for the first time glanced back at her over his shoulder.

"I think we can cross," he called and there was a

distorted echo from below uttering his words so garbled they might have been from the throat of some beast. "It seems to continue. Let me see the other end."

"Well enough." Elossa dropped down just beyond the edge of the face, watching as he once more advanced slowly but steadily ahead. Around her the dark thickened as the torch was carried farther and farther away. She could hardly make out the details of the tongue passage, save that it seemed to her that it was narrowing to an extent where Stans might not even find width enough to support both knees at once.

The Raski's advance was very slow. Though he held the torch up to illuminate as much as he could of what still stretched before him, his other hand grasped the edge of the bridge in a grip Elossa did not have to see clearly to realize was tightened by the very real presence of fear. Then he moved so that now his legs dropped, one on either side of that path which had become so narrow his own body more than spanned it.

He began to hitch, his legs swinging over nothingness. Elossa, without being conscious of what she did, pressed one fist against her mouth, until the pain in her pinched lips made her aware. The torch had certainly not caught any sign yet of the other side of the chasm. What if the tongue became a tip and Stans slid off it into the depths?

The malice of the carven face certainly promised no more than harsh disaster for anyone daring to trust to it. She longed to shout to the Raski to return, but at the same time feared that any sudden summons might send him off balance, to fall.

She blinked, hardly sure that she did see that hint of a ledge of rock reaching out toward the tongue tip from the far side. Was there a space between the two which could not in the end be bridged? Or did the very tip of the stone span actually rest upon the ledge? It was too far—the light too confined by the distance—for her to make sure. Her heart was pounding, she had risen to her knees, staring out at that small flicker of flame which was so perilously distant.

Stans made a convulsive movement—a fall! Her breath caught in a choking gasp. No! He was getting to his feet, and now the torch was swinging back and forth like the flag of a victorious army waved to signal triumph.

He started back, down once more on the thread of stone, edging along, holding the torch before him. Her own body ached with tension as she watched him make the slow return trip. She only breathed deeply and fully once more when he arose to walk the last few steps to gain the lips of the face from which that incredible bridge issued.

"Is is very narrow toward the end. . . ." He breathed in short gasps and in the torchlight she could well see the sheen of sweat across his face. That journey had not been an easy one. "There is but a very small margin of meeting between bridge and the edge on the far side. But it is a crossing."

"As you have proved." She tried to make her face impassive. There was no escape save this very risky path. All her life she had known mountain trails which were narrow, where one must walk with the greatest of care, the highest dependence upon one's balance and skill. Yet the worst of those was as nothing compared to the ordeal before her now. She needs must shut away fear, and with it that other feeling of repugnance for the form of their only escape. To her the face carried such a sensation of sheer evil that to trust her body to the tongue was nearly more than she could force herself to do. The thing was stone, it had no life—except that illusion it might be able to foster in those who feared it—yet there was deep in her a sick hatred born from the need to touch its substance.

A picture haunted her, a vision of the tongue curling up and around, as that tongue of fog had wreathed the Raski. A stone tongue to hold her securely a prisoner, draw her back into the gaping mouth of. . . .

Elossa shook her head. To allow such a vision any place in her mind was to carry out the very purposes of those who had created Atturn—whatever he was. She held her head high and was pleased that her voice was so steady as she asked:

"How do we go?"

Stans had been looking back along the path he had taken once.

"I think I go first—if we only had a rope!"

Elossa managed a laugh which did not sound too ragged. "Uniting us? To what purpose in disaster save that it would mean the loss of us both then. I do not believe that either of us could sustain the weight of the other were that one to slip. If it must be done, let us get to the doing of it!" Perhaps with that last outburst she had revealed her dismay. If so he did not let her realize, by even a look, that he knew how fear ate at her.

Instead, holding the torch close enough to him that the light shone well over his shoulder, he set forth with an air of steady confidence to again cross the tongue. Staff in hand her cloak held tightly about her, Elossa followed.

It seemed only too soon that they must descend from walking to crawling on hands and knees. She tried to keep her eyes only for the stone way that the flame showed. But those edges drawing ever more closely together were a torment to watch. Maybe she was lucky in that complete darkness did fill the chasm. Was it better not to see? Only then imagination could paint what the eyes did not distinguish.

"Astride here," his words floated back.

Elossa hitched high her robe, bunching it about her waist. The stone, rough and cold, chafed the skin of her inner thighs as she edged slowly along, and the perch on which she rested grew ever more narrow. Her dangling legs appeared to gather weight, making her ever afraid of over-balancing.

Then Stans seemed to give a leap, if one could so express his quick thrust forward from a sitting position. The torch flashed down. He had laid its butt on a ledge, the flame out over the gulf. On his knees, he turned to reach both hands to hers.

Somehow the girl loosed her grip on the stone. The staff she had held across her lap she snatched up, angling it to him. He seized the length of wood, then there came a steady pull, to drag her over what was indeed the most shaky of supports—the very tip of the tongue, a bit of stone no wider than her hand, where it just touched the ledge.

She sprawled forward, her body landing full on

Stans, pushing him back across the stone. For a moment or two she could not move at all. It was as if the demands she had put on her body and her courage had weakened both at once leaving her as weak and empty as one who has been ill for a long time.

Stans' arms closed about her. She was hardly aware of that fastidious dislike for touching another which was so much a part of her heritage. Elossa only knew at this moment the warmth of his body close against hers sent rushing back into the darkness of the gulf all the fear which had gnawed at her. They were across—there was stable rock under them.

Then the Raski loosed her as he made a lunge for the torch which was sputtering. He swung it up through the air so the flames took on new life. Elossa felt tears runneling the rock dust on her cheeks, but she bit back any sound. Using the staff for a support she was able to drag herself up and stand, though it felt to her for some space out of time that the solid rock which was her footing swayed from side to side.

Stans, torch in hand, held out that brand. There was no mistaking the way those flames were borne back toward them. Just as the current of air, which seemed to her as fresh as the wind from a mountain tip, blew from some space before them. There must be some way out waiting for them.

Elossa was hungry, her body ached from the journey. But she was in no mind to suggest that they halt, drink of what they carried in the water bottles strapped to their girdles, or eat the rest of her crumbs of journey bread. If there was a chance of winning out of here in the not too distant future, that was all that mattered.

The size of ledge on which they stood did have limits. It might not be as clearly defined as the tongue for a bridge, but there was space to be seen on either side. Only, before them loomed a new opening in a rock wall, unworked natural stone. It was down this passage that the air came.

Stans had thrown back his head, was drawing in deep breaths.

"We must be close to the outer world," he commented. "There is no underground taint in this wind."

He must feel as heartened by the thought of escape as she was for he moved on with a hasty stride and she hurried to catch up with him.

14

They emerged into a night near as dark as the passage from which they came. Clouds massed overhead heavily enough to shut out all signs of moon or stars. And there was a wind which carried in it more than a promise of the winter season now not so distant. Having found their door they were not so determined to use it yet, at least not until they knew more of the world into which they had come. In mutual consent they withdrew again into the passage and, finding a niche which protected them somewhat from the wind, they crowded into its shelter, deciding to wait out the hours of dark there.

Elossa brought out the last of her journey cakes—a mass of crumbs. And they had the water in the bottles. Having eaten, they drank, and then agreed, though they lacked any method of telling time, to share sentry duties.

Stans arbitrarily claimed the first watch period and

Elossa did not dispute him. The ordeal of the bridge crossing still was with her. She was content for now to huddle within her cloak and just rest. But sleep came upon her then with the suddenness of a blow.

When she roused from that state it was to feel Stans' hand on her shoulder, shaking her into wakefulness. He grunted some disjointed words she did not clearly catch and settled down himself in the dark leaving her to look out upon the strangeness of this over-mountain country.

At first she sharpened her sleep-drugged wits by trying to place their present position. Their crossing of the valley had been mainly an east to west trail. But when Stans had sought the Mouth he had certainly gone north. Had their journey also within the interior of the heights been northward? She was certain that was so. As her eyes adjusted to the dark she believed that they were surrounded by peaks higher than the foothills among which they had earlier traveled. There was no mistaking a certain feel to which she was sensitive from her life among the heights.

Now that the pressure of the journey, the need to escape, was gone, she tried to marshal what little she knew, what she had observed and felt, into a logical sequence from which she might reason possible future action.

Two heritages had been very much in evidence in the way of the Mouth: Raski—even though Stans denied that he knew much of Atturn—Yurth in the mysterious figure who had attempted to slay them with the ancient weapon of her own people and then had vanished.

Yet because of their very heritage there was no

reasonable motive for such a melding of menace. Until she and Stans had stood in the sky ship and made their own uneasy alliance there had been, to Elossa's knowledge, no pacific meeting between Yurth and Raski.

She fumbled in folds of her clothing and brought forth the mirror pendant. There was no light of moon to give it life; she was able to see only a disc, and that very shadowy in her hand. Also to use that would open her mind, leave her defenseless to any other who had mind-send, mind-probe. Restlessly she fingered it, longing to put it to use caution acting as a brake on her desire.

That Yurth call—concerning that she had *not* been mistaken. If that were only a mental illusion, to match what had been visual ones, then she was indeed lost. A chill of fear crawled along her body, far worse than any cold brought by the wind and the stone surrounding her. Mind must control illusion. But if the mind itself were to be invaded by such— against that not even the most strongly armed Yurth could stand! And she did not claim the completely trained powers of her elders.

She raised the half-seen mirror to her lips, breathed upon it. Then holding it at eye level she concentrated. Yurth—if there was Yurth here then that call would bring, should bring. . . .

Elossa could see the disc only as an object between her fingers. She had never tried before to use it in such an absence of light. There was—no, she was not mistaken! The disc grew warm—it was activated!

Yurth! Urgently she beamed out that call.

No answer, though she put into her mind-send all

the strength she could summon. If Yurth had ever been here then her people were now gone. Dare she try Raski? As Elossa hesitated, the memory of the Mouth was sharp in her mind. Better not play with forces she did not understand. That looping shadow tongue which had near taken Stans was something beyond her own knowledge. Regretfully she clasped the mirror between her palms, loosed all concentration, then stowed it carefully away.

There was a lighting of the sky beginning, and, judging by that, they were indeed facing north. How long did they have before the first storms of the cold season would close in? Though the Yurth had their log huts and stone caves, their storage houses, yet that season was never easy for them. She and Stans had no supplies, no shelter as yet. Both must now be their primary concern.

Dawn broke at last and Elossa could see the new land lying below, for the passage in which they had sheltered part of the night fronted on a slope well above the floor of a valley. Unlike the wide expanse which had held the destroyed city, this was relatively narrow. But it ran east and west and she was sure that she caught a glimpse of a stream of some size forming a ribbon down its center. There was growth of dark vegetation on the lower slopes, rising to stunted trees. But there was something unwholesome about the look of that.

Still a source of water was important. Only, where there was any stream, they could also expect to find a come and go of life. Sargon, such as had already near made an end to her over mountain, and kindred beasts of the heights might well roam here. Stans carried a hunter's weapons, she had nothing save her staff. Nor had she ever taken life herself.

"Darksome. . . ." Stans moved out to join her. "This is no country to welcome the traveler. Yet there is water. So it may well be good hunting territory."

They left the entrance to the tunnel to proceed down slope. Without any spoken agreement they both made good use of all cover as they went, while Elossa opened her mind a little, striving to pick up any hint of life.

"Two-horns—" She spoke in a whisper gauged just to reach the ears of the man moving hardly an arm's distance away.

He shot her a startled glance.

"To the west." She pointed with her chin. "There are four—they graze."

He nodded swiftly and turned in the direction she had indicated. His crossbow was in his hands. Elossa felt a little sick. At least she had not tolled a helpless animal within striking distance. But her betrayal was little the less. How true was it that one was allowed to slay in order to live? She could defend herself against attack—but a two horn was no attacker. She. . . . No, in this much she must face the necessity of breaking her own creed. To starve because one would not kill—a stronger person might face that rule, she fell far short of such strength.

Also since this was of her doing, she must force herself to watch. So, like Stans, she slipped along.

The brush which cloaked the slope gave way to a stand of grass which waved tips near as tall as the shoulders of the animals who grazed there. Four two-horns. Elossa had read the emanations of life forces aright. There was one female, a half-grown yearling, and two males—one with the wide-curved horns of a herd leader of more than ten seasons.

Stans shot. The younger male gave a convulsive leap forward a red stream shooting from its throat. The other male cried aloud in a great bellow and herded the female and her yearling before him into flight. The wounded animal had fallen to its knees as the bolt in its jugular drained it of blood. Stans raced on, knife in hand, to swiftly end its struggles.

Sick at what she had seen, Elossa made herself advance to where the Raski was busy butchering the kill. She stooped and thrust her fingers into the congealing blood. Then she drew on her forehead the scarlet sign of her sin. So must she wear that for all to note until in some manner she might atone. She looked around to see the Raski, pausing in his bloody work, watching her action with open amazement.

"It is through me the innocent had died," she said, not wanting to explain her shame, but knowing that she must. "So must I wear a killer's blood token."

His surprise did not lighten. "This is meat, we must have it or die. There are no fields to be harvested here, no fruit ripe for the picking. Do not the Yurth eat meat? If not so, how do they live?"

"We live," she said bleakly. "And we kill. But never must we let ourselves forget that in killing we take on ever the burden which is part of the death of another, be it man or animal."

"You did not blood yourself with the sargon," he commented.

"No, for then the fight was equal—life risked against life—and that is left upon the balance of the First Principle, not upon any better skill or trick of ours."

Stans shook his head and his expression was still one of bafflement.

"Yurth ways—" He shrugged. "It remains, we can eat."

"Dare we light a fire?" The girl looked on to the end of the meadow which bordered on the stream. Across that swift flow of water (and it was swift, bearing with it sticks, masses of wrack as if there had been a storm somewhere higher up and the hurrying flood had picked up much debris along the way) there were standing rocks and sand, none of the vegetation which grew on this side.

"What do your Yurth talents tell you?" he countered. "If you can so find a beast to give us food without searching far, can you not also tell us whether we are alone here?" He sat back on his heels, his face impassive.

Elossa could not be really convinced whether he asked that without latent hostility. They were so different in their heritage—dare she ever be certain that there did not lie some other motive under any speech he made to her?

She hesitated. To reveal her weaknesses when she could not be sure of this Raski—that might be the height of stupidity. Yet she must not, on the other hand, claim powers which in a time of emergency she could not summon. That might well be worse in the future than admitting now there were limits to what she could do.

"If I use such a mind-search," Elossa said slowly, "and there is a mind equally trained within range, then instantly that other will know of me—or us."

"It would be a Yurth mind which could do so, would it not?" he asked. "Do you then fear your own people?"

"I travel with a Raski." She picked the first excuse she could light upon. "They do not hate nor fear your kind, but I would be so strange because of that."

"Yes, even as I company with Yurth!" He nodded. "Most of my own blood would send such a bolt as this—" He touched what he had taken from the wound—"through me without question."

She made her decision, mainly for the reason that hunger was strong in her; still she could not think of putting raw flesh into her mouth. A poor reason, in which the needs of her body overrode all else, yet the body must be fed or the mind also would perish.

Kneeling a little away from where Stans had gone back to his butchery, Elossa again brought out her mirror. The sun was up now, and the surface of the disc she held was bright as it had not been in the night time. She looked down into the pool of light, for that was what it seemed to become in her hold.

"Yurth!" She aimed the thought sharply into the disc. "Show me Yurth!"

There was—yes! It came—a rippling on the surface of the disc. Then she saw—but very faint and hard to define—a figure which might have been that which had fronted them in the corridor. Her mind-send reached out and out. Life . . . far. . . . But was it Yurth? She met no answering spark of mind. It was more like Raski—closed, unknowing.

"There is nothing close." She slipped the disc back into its carrying place.

"Good enough. There is drift along the stream—dry enough to give us a good fire, and also that which will not cause much smoke."

Leaving him to finish his bloody task, Elossa went down to the water and began to gather those bone-white, water-polished sticks which had caught in the rocks above the present rise of the water, though, she noted, that was creeping higher now even as she watched.

They roasted chunks of the meat speared on sharpened pieces of drift and held over the flames. Elossa forced herself to eat, applying mental discipline against her half nausea. Stans was licking his fingers one by one as he spoke disjointedly:

"We should smoke what we can—to carry with us."

He had said only that when Elossa was on her feet, staring across the stream at the other rock-covered bank. Just as the strange Yurth and the face had both appeared without warning in the passage, so now had a figure winked into sight there.

She gasped. Not Yurth as she had half expected. Like Stans the man was dark-skinned, dark haired. But—his face! He wore a living countenance of flesh and bone but it was still the one of Atturn. Nor was his clothing the hide garments of the hunter, even the clumsy ill-woven robes of the city men, or the primitive armor of the Raski soldiers who patrolled the plains.

His body was covered with a black, tight-fitting suit, not unlike those worn by the Yurth in their shipboard life, save that the black was scrolled over by patterns in red as if so drawn by some point dipped in fresh blood. Those patterns glowed, waned, and glowed again, their brightness speeding from one part of the body they helped to clothe to another. From his shoulders hung a short cloak of the blood red, and that was patterned in black, reversing the order of that on his other clothing. His head was surmounted by a towering crest of either thick black hair set in some invisible helm, or else his own locks stiffened and allowed to grow to a height of more than a foot above his skull. In all he was the most barbaric figure Elossa had ever seen.

Instinctively she had sent forth a mind-probe. And met—nothing.

The stranger raised his hand and pointed, while his lips—the thickish, sneering lips of the Mouth of Atturn—shaped words which sounded heavily through the air as if the words themselves were bolts from some weapon dispatched to bring down the two on the other side of the river.

"Raski, *si lar dit!*"

Stans cried out. The appearance of the man had caught him kneeling now he was on his feet in a half crouch, his hand tightly grasping the hilt of his knife. Like the stranger who wore Atturn's face his features were alive, but his expression was that of defiance.

"Philbur!" He made of the name of his house a battle cry. It was as if he met red hate with a rage as great and overpowering.

Without clear thought Elossa's hand grabbed her mirror from its hiding place, the swift jerk of her pull breaking the cord which held it. Then, swinging it by what was left of that cord, she spun it through the air.

Was what happened then chance alone or some intervention of power she did not realize she could call upon? A beam of searing red fire had shot from the pointed finger of he who wore Atturn's face. It struck full on the disc of the mirror and was reflected back—its force of beam increased. The black and red figure vanished.

15

"Who was that?" Elossa found words first, Stans was still staring bemused at where that stranger had stood.

"It was—no!" He flung up one hand in an emphatic gesture of denial. "It could not be that!" Now he turned his head a little to look at the girl and his look of astonishment was still plain. "Time does not stop—a man dead these half thousand years cannot walk!"

"Walk." She gazed at the mirror which had so providently, almost impossibly, deflected whatever it was the stranger would have hurled at Stans. The disc was cracked, darkened. A vigorous rubbing against her cloak did not free it from that discoloration. Without even trying it she could be sure it was now useless for her purposes. "Walk," she repeated explosively, "that strove to kill!" For Elossa did not doubt in the least that had that beam of light struck

Stans he would have been as dead as she would have been had the Yurth weapon in the corridor cooked her flesh from her charred bones.

"It was Karn of the House of Philbur—he who ruled in Kal-Hath-Tan. He is—was—of my blood, or I of his. But he died with the city! It is so—all men know it! Yet, you saw him, did you not? Tell me—" His voice was near a fierce shout—"you did see him!"

"I saw a man—a Raski if you say he is so—in black and red, but he wore the face of the Mouth of Atturn and you said you did not know it."

Stans rubbed his hand across his forehead. He was visibly more shaken than she had yet seen him.

"I know—what do I know—or not know?" He cried that question, not to her, she knew, but to the world around them. "I am no longer sure of anything."

Then he took a leap in her direction, and, before the girl could move, he had seized her shoulders in a hurtful grip and was shaking her as if he would so reduce her to a kind of slavery.

"Was this of your doing, Yurth? All know you can tangle and play with minds, as a true man can toss pebbles to his liking. Have you so tossed my thoughts, bewitched my eyes—made me see what is not?"

The girl fought him, tearing herself free by the very fury of her resistance. Then she backed away, holding up to him at eye level the blackened and near destroyed mirror of seeing.

"He did that—with the beam that he threw! Think you, Raski, how would you have been served had this not deflected that power!"

Stans' scowl did not lighten but his eyes did flicker at the disc.

"I do not know what he would have done," he said sullenly. "This is an evil land and—"

He got no further. They came boiling out of the rocks across the water, splashing through, some of them covering the distance between with huge leaps. Not Yurth, not Raski. . . . Elossa gave a cry of horror, so alien were these creatures to any normal life that she knew.

Twisted bodies, limbs too long or too short, heads with horribly misshapen features—a nightmare of distorted things which vaguely aped the human yet were totally monstrous. It was this alien horror which kept both Elossa and Stans from instant defense. Also the creatures attacked without a sound, surging on in a wave over the water toward them.

Elossa stopped to catch up her staff; Stans still had his hunting knife to hand. But they had no chance. Evil smelling bodies ringed them in, hands which had four fingers, six, boneless tentacles for digits, seized upon them, dragged them down. The terrible revulsion which filled Elossa as she looked upon their distorted and deformed bodies and faces weakened her. She fought, but it was as if nausea weighted her limbs, deadened her powers of constructive thought.

They poured over the two by the fire like an irresistible wave, bearing them to earth. Elossa shuddered at the touch of their unwholesome flesh against her own. The fetid odor they wore like a second skin made it hard for her to breathe, she had to fight to regain consciousness. There were bonds pulled cruelly

tight about her wrists and ankles. Still one of the creatures squatted on her, using the force of its weight to keep her quiet.

And the worst of that (Elossa had to close her eyes against the horror of that leering, drooling thing) was that it was obviously female. For their attackers wore but little clothing—scraps of filthy stuff about their loins the extent of their body coverings, the females among them as aggressive and bestial as the males.

The silence in which their attack had been carried out was broken now. Grunts, whistles, noises not even as intelligent as sounds made by far more cleanly living animals broke out in an unintelligible chorus.

Elossa, the center of one circle of captors, could see nothing of the Raski. She forced herself to look at these ringing her in. While they indulged meanwhile in small torments, pulling viciously at her hair, tweaking her flesh until the nails—of those which had nails—near met, leaving raw marks which bled a little.

There appeared to be, she began to understand, some argument in progress among them. Twice one party of the creatures strove to drag her away from the river, while others jabbered and screamed and fought over her to bring her back.

She waited for the man named Karn to appear, somehow sure that he must have been the one to unleash on them this frightful band. But there was no one but the things themselves. One had thrust a stick into the fire, whirled it around in the air until the end blazed and now limped, for one of its legs was shorter than the other, toward her, the fiery point manifestly aimed at her eyes.

Before that reached the goal the would-be torturer was tackled by a much taller and heavier male, whose tentacle fingers fastened about its fellow's thin, corded throat and dragged him back, flinging him away with callous force.

Before the jabbering creature could reclaim its stick there was a sharp outcry from those nearest the river. Now the large male waded into those about Elossa cuffing with fists, kicking out with feet on which there were no toes, growling hoarsely.

Having battered near half of her captors away, the male stooped and caught at a great handful of her hair. By this painful hold he dragged her to the water's edge. Then, seizing her by the middle of her body, he raised and flung her out.

She did not land in the water, but rather in some kind of a boat which rocked perilously under her weight, but did not turn over. A moment later Stans landed half on top of her, hurled in the same manner.

The Raski lay so limp Elossa feared he was dead. His weight across her body forced her into the bottom of the boat where there was a wash of slimy water. She had to struggle to lift her head so that would not lap into her face.

Under them the boat lurched and then floated free. But none of the horrors on the shore made move to join the prisoners in it. They were being sent alone, bound and helpless, into the full force of the current. Elossa's struggles made the boat rock dangerously. But she had achieved a few inches of room which did just keep her face above the water.

Caught in what was indeed a swift current, the boat rode dizzily, sometimes spinning half around.

Much of Elossa's range of sight was curtailed by Stans' body. She could really see only straight up where the sky held a thin, promising sunlight. But, as they were borne along, walls began to rise on either side, those same walls closing in toward the river. They cut off much of the sky. All she could soon see was a strip forming a ribbon between two towering stretches of dark rock.

The sound of rushing water was ever present. Now and then the boat grated against some obstruction beyond Elossa's curtailed range of sight and she waited tensely for their craft to rip apart on a sunken stone, or be overturned, allowing them to drown. Meanwhile she struggled against the cords about her wrists. Those were well under the water which washed in the boat and she wondered if the continued immersion might loosen the ties. But she was afraid to fight too hard lest her movements endanger the bouyancy of their clumsy craft.

A groan from Stans heartened her a little. Perhaps if he could regain consciousness they might have a slightly better chance. Then she saw the seeping of blood from his shoulder. That nearly healed wound which he had carried from his brush with the first sargon must have been wrenched open once again.

"Stans!" She called his name.

A second groan answered her. Then a muttering which was near lost in the sound of the water. Imagination was busy nibbling at the grip she held tight upon her emotions. Given the swiftness of the current here what might well lie ahead? Rapids which no such leaky craft as this could hope to ride, or even a waiting cataract or falls?

"Stans!" Perhaps she was wrong in trying to arouse the Raski—what if he should make some sudden move which would overbalance them?

But the water was washing higher now. It flicked in small waves against her chin. If he did not shift his weight in some manner she would be past the ability to keep her face above its surface much longer.

His body did move a fraction and the boat dipped. The water swirled up and she choked as it entered her nose without warning.

"Be—be quiet!" Her voice arose nearly to a shriek in her fear.

"Where. . . ." His voice was weak, she thought, but it sounded as if he were conscious.

"We are in a boat." She tried to outtalk the river sounds. "I am partly beneath you. There is water here. I must keep my face above it."

Had he understood? He made no immediate answer. She tried to wriggle away from him to the bow of the boat, hold her head up. Her neck ached and it was becoming more and more difficult to do that.

Then his words came clearly enough. "I shall try to move away," he said. "Be ready!"

She braced herself, took a deep breath to have her lungs full if she were to be ducked. His weight did move, slid a little down her body toward the stern of the boat. That rocked wildly under them, and the waves she feared did wash over her face. But through some favor of providence the craft did not overset.

Once more he moved. And then she felt free. Now it was her turn.

"Be ready," she warned. "I shall try to edge away, get my shoulders higher."

After a fashion she did. Her chin was jammed down into her chest, but the water was now well away from her face. Also she could see that he, in turn, was wedged across the boat in part, his head and shoulders against one side, his legs and knees trailing down the other.

The current was still fast but the boat seemed to ride it a little more steadily. Elossa knew very little of boats; they were never used by the Yurth. Perhaps their changes of position had something to do with the alteration.

From her present place she could see that the river must fill a very narrow gap between two very steep banks. It was as if they passed so through a mountain canyon. Even if they were free, and managed somehow to get out of the water she greatly doubted that there was any way either of those natural walls could be climbed.

Once more she cautiously tried the ties about her wrists. And, to her overwhelming excitement they gave a little. The water's soaking must have helped. She passed her discovery to Stans. He nodded, but it did not seem to interest him. Under the darkness of his skin there was a greenish color. His eyes closed as if it was beyond his strength to keep them open, and he lay inert. It might have taken all the energy he could summon to have made the move which freed her.

But her own determination and will were growing stronger. The extreme effect of those horrible attackers had faded. Alone, bound and helpless though they seemed to be, she could begin to search for some hope. To get her hands free—that was what she must first do.

In spite of the pain in her wrists, she flexed and relaxed, flexed and relaxed, tugging at intervals, though that repaid her with torment in her flayed skin.

Stans continued to lie with closed eyes and the girl believed that he had again lapsed into unconsciousness. She wondered how long their voyage down the river would continue. She was able to force her head up another few inches to see that once more the walls of the cut through which they were traveling were beginning to descend—the cliffs were not so tall and forbidding.

A last effort and she jerked one hand free. Her puffed fingers had no feeling in them. Then the agony of returning circulation made her want to scream aloud. She forced herself to flex those swollen hands in spite of the pain. But she could also use them to lever herself up cautiously farther in the boat, release her head and neck from the strain put upon them.

Though it was hard to make her fingers obey with any success she picked at the ties around her ankles. The thongs had cut deeply there and puffed rings showed bloody. Then she remembered that the creatures who had taken them captive had not searched her. And, using both hands together, she hunted within the bosom of her robe for that concealed pocket where she carried the small knife to serve her at meals.

It nearly fell through her nerveless fingers, but she managed to saw away at the thongs. As soon as those parted she edged warily around to see what she could do for Stans. Sitting up in the boat she had a better view of the river. Here it was much narrower than it had been in the valley, which might well add to the speed of the current.

The boat itself was blunt bowed, rising high on the sides. It appeared to be made of a wooden frame over which was tight stretched hide so thick it must come from some beast beyond Yurth knowledge. That was also scaled on the outside as she could see where it had been brought over at the edge and laced down. And she did not doubt that it was perhaps far tougher than any wood.

There was a feeling of age about it, as if not of her time at all. And she marveled at how bouyantly it rode.

Using both hands she shifted Stans a little, with a catch of breath as the boat dipped ominously. But at least she was able to saw at the cords near buried in the flesh of his wrists where they had been drawn so cruelly tight.

His ankles had fared better than hers for he wore the boots of a hunter. And there was more give to the bonds there. Once he was free she settled him as best she could to steady the boat. The blood stains from his shoulder had not spread, she could hope that the wound had stopped bleeding.

Now—without any oar, paddle, or means of controlling their craft—what could be done to better their present state? Elossa drew a deep breath as she turned her attention back to the river.

16

She did not have long to wonder for the end of their wild voyage was very near. The higher walls about them sank swiftly, until they came out of the canyon into another valley—if valley it was and not a plains country beyond the mountains. At least this level land, clothed in the autumn hued grass, spread as far on out as Elossa could distinguish ahead.

The river which carried them did not flow so swiftly here, and its way across the plain was marked by stands of water-nourished brush and small trees which were the only vegetation to rise above the level of the thick grass. For the rest this seemed a deserted land. It was close to sunset as far as Elossa could judge and there was not a bird to be seen, no grazing animals in sight.

While the dull hue of the grass and the faded colors of the tree leaves gave a forbidding cast to the whole of this land, it appeared as if all vibrant life had been drawn out of it, and only withered remnants left. Looking around she shivered, more from inner than outer chill.

A groan from Stans drew her attention back to her companion. His eyes were open and he had shifted his position a little. When his gaze met hers it was plain he realized at least some of what had happened.

With his hand he touched his shoulder carefully and winced. But at least he was fully conscious. Now he looked out at the plain into which the river was carrying them.

"We are beyond the heights." It was more a statement than a question.

"Yes," Elossa answered. "Though where we may be I have no idea."

He was frowning and now he rubbed his hand across his forehead. "Was it a dream—or did we see Karn back there?"

Elossa chose her words. "We saw a man . . . he had a face like the Mouth of Atturn . . . you called him Karn."

"Then it was not just a dream." Stans spoke heavily. "But Karn is long dead. Though, yes, he was priest as well as king and in his own time men whispered behind their hands—a dark legend but one even I have heard remnants of. Karn dealt with forces most men did not even believe existed. Or so they say—and said. It is true I cannot remember clearly." Now he shook his head. "I feel that I should, but that some wall stands between me and the truth. Karn. . . ." his voice trailed away.

"If that was your long dead king," Elossa cut in sharply, "he has taken to himself some evil followers. The monsters who brought us down were no true living men.''

"Yes. And them, of them I have no knowledge at all. But why they loosed us to the mercy of the river and this boat. . . .'' He moved again and his face twisted with what must have been a grievous twinge of pain. But he had hitched up farther and was gazing around as if now intent upon assessing their situation clearly.

"No oars," he commented. "It is plain we are not meant to command any part of the future. But. . . .''

Elossa, who had looked back at the river and what lay ahead, gave an exclamation. There seemed to be a wall of brush now directly above the water, though that flowed unimpeded beneath it. It was evident that bearing down upon the barrier as they were, there was no other chance but that the boat would be brought up against it.

Carefully she got to her knees, balancing with difficulty as the boat bobbed and moved under her weight. Even if she stood, Elossa guessed, she could not have reached the top of that obstruction across the water.

The boat rocked again as Stans raised himself higher. He gestured to the river itself.

"Swim for it?" he suggested.

Though Elossa had splashed about in mountain pools she knew that she would be at a loss in this current-driven river. She hesitated. Perhaps, were they to bring up against the mass of the barrier, that could be better climbed. Yet the presence of the barrier itself was an implied threat. It had not simply appeared there as some freak of nature, of that she was sure. Made—it brought to mind the question of its makers and the purpose for which they might have erected it.

In the end they were given no choice at all. For even as the boat neared the barrier, there dropped, seemingly from the very air over their heads (though Elossa knew it must be the result of some well trained casting) a net which entangled both the boat and its occupants.

She and Stans were fighting that entrapment when those who had so arranged their capture appeared out of the brush and trees on either side of the stream. Unlike the misshapen monsters of their first encounter with the mountain dwellers, these were straight of body, well formed. And—they were Yurth!

Elossa cried out for help. These were kin, her own blood. But—were they. Some wore the coarse clothing of the mountain clans, enough like her own to have come from the same looms. Others had on the tight-fitting body suits she had seen in the pictures the ship had shown her, the same that Yurth who had aimed the ancient weapon at them scarce a day ago had appeared in.

Elossa sent out an imperative mind-call. To be so startled in return that she cried out. These were closed—tight guarded against her touch. Yurth they might appear in body—they were not Yurth in mind.

Also she saw now their faces more clearly—they were blank eyed, without expression. Nor did they speak to one another in any words as these on the left bank drew the net and so the boat and its two occupants toward them.

"Yurth," Stans said. "Your people—what would they do with us?"

Elossa shook her head. She felt so strange and at a loss—meeting closed minds, blank faces where she had the right to expect something far different—that she now had the sensation of being caught tight in some nightmare, or else laid under so strong a hallucination that it endured in spite of any attempt on her part to break it.

"They look Yurth—" She spoke her bewilderment aloud. "But they are not, not the Yurth I know."

If they were not her people, they were well used to handling prisoners taken in their odd net and water trap. And there were too many of them for either Elossa or Stans, weakened as he was by the reopening of his wound, to put up any defense. Even though her first attempt at communication had failed, the girl tried twice again to launch mind-send at their captors. But it would seem that none were receptive.

In the end, their hands once more bound behind them, she and Stans were marched away from the river and the boat, now tied at the bank, striking out across the dull emptiness of the plain. At sunset they camped where a circle of stones set to confine fire to a much blackened and ash-piled piece of ground suggested that this was a well used halting place.

The Yurth had marched in silence, speaking neither to their prisoners nor each other. Elossa had come to feel a shrinking from contact with any of them. They might well be only hollow shells of the people she had known, sent to obey the will of some other, without a spirit of their own remaining in their bodies.

At least those bodies remained human in their need for food and water. For supplies were produced and shared with their prisoners, unbound for the purpose, but watched closely while they gnawed on lengths of what seemed dried meat, as hard to chew as wood, and allowed to drink from journey bottles. Even the water had a strange, stale taste as if it had been in those storage containers for a long time.

"Where do you take us?" In the general silence of that camp Stans' voice rang out unusually loud. He had spoken to the Yurth who was rebinding his hands.

The man might have been deaf for he did not even glance up as he tested the last knot with grim efficiency before he turned away. Now the Raski looked to Elossa.

"They are of your stock, surely they will answer you." There was an odd note in his voice. Almost, Elossa thought, as if he had already identified her wholly with his enemies in spite of the outward trappings of captivity which she wore.

She moistened her lips and launched the one appeal she had thought upon during that dusty journey to reach this place. To do this before a Raski went against all her conditioning from birth—Yurth affairs were theirs only. Still she must break through to these of her kin; that need had become the most important thing in her whole world.

Again she ran her tongue over her lips; her mouth, in spite of the water she had drunk, felt bone dry, as if she could not shape any words.

But this must be done—she had to *know*. So she began to chant in words so old that even their meaning was now forgotten. Out of some very dim past

had those words come, and their birth must have
been of abiding importance to all which was Yurth
for the fact still remained that they must learn them,
intelligible or no.

"In the beginning," she said in that tongue now
forgotten, "was created Heaven and Yurth," (that
last was the only understandable word in her chant),
"and there man took being and. . . ."

On sped the words, faster now and uttered with
more power and authority. And—yes! One of the
Yurth, one wearing the clothing like her own, had
turned his head to look at her. There was the faint
trace of puzzlement dawning in his blank face. She
saw his lips move. Then his voice joined hers in the
chant, lower, less strong, halting at times.

But when she had done he saw her, really saw her!
It was as if she had shaken out of sleep this one, if
not the others. His eyes swept from her face down to
the wrists again bound, the end of that cording looping out to twist about the arm of another of the
guards. The attention in his expression became
hopelessness.

"To Yurth the burden of the Sin." He spoke
harshly as might a man who had not used his voice
for a long time. "We pay, Yurth, we pay."

She leaned forward. None of the others had appeared to note that he had spoken.

"To whom does Yurth pay?" She tried to keep her
voice as level as might one carrying on a usual
conversation.

"To Atturn." His last faint trace of interest flickered out. Now he turned away and got to his feet.

She sent a mind-probe with all the force she could

summon, determined to break through the barrier she had found, to reach the real man within the shell. Maybe she troubled him a fraction, for his head did turn once more in her direction. Then he strode off into the growing dusk.

"So Yurth pays," commented Stans.

"To Atturn," she snapped in return, desolated at her failure when she had begun to think that she might have actually learned more. "Perhaps to your Karn." She ended, not because she believed what she said. "But if Atturn rules, why does a Raski go in bonds?" she flung at him in conclusion.

"Perhaps we shall soon have a chance to learn." He showed heat to match her own.

With the dark the Yurth settled themselves for sleep, each captive placed carefully between two of their guards, cords looping them in contact so that Elossa guessed that the least move on her part would alert either one or the other, or both, of the men who boxed her in. He who had spoken to her was across the fire and settled early, his eyes closed, as if the last thing he wanted to see was Elossa herself.

She slept at last, rousing once to see one of the Yurth feeding the fire from a pile of sticks which had been stacked there waiting for their coming. Stans was only a dark form nearly engulfed in the shadows and she could not tell whether he waked or slept.

There was an uneasiness in her now which made her adverse to any casting of mind-seek. That these Yurth were perhaps bound to another's will was the only explanation which made sense to her. The "Burden" which the ship had loosed on her had ridden her people heavily for generations, that was true. But that it had reduced any to this state was not normal—Yurth normal. He and the others who had worn the clothing like her own—were they those who had earlier made the Pilgrimage and had never returned? Instead of death in the mountains they had found this life-in-death.

But there were the others who wore the ship's clothing. It had certainly been too many years since the crash of their spacer and the death of Kal-Hath-Tan for any of them to have lived to this time—again, unless someone had found the secret of prolonging life far past any scale of years known to Elossa's reckoning. Had there been another ship, a later one?

There was such a surge of excitement through her at that thought that she had to will herself fiercely to lie still. It was the same excitement and racing of the blood which had visited her when she had watched in the wrecked ship the scenes taken in space before the crash.

Another ship—a later one—perhaps sent to find Yurth, to take them home. Home? Where was home then? Lying here she could see the stars strewn across the sky. Was one of them the sun which warmed the fields and hills of Yurth Home?

She drew a deep breath and then that excitement changed.

Those around her, she knew they were not free. If they had come to save, then they in turn had been caught in some trap and made captive. Yet they could not have been conditioned by the machines in the ship as all those of her own blood and kin had been. She longed to be able to crawl over to Stans, to shake him awake if he did indeed sleep, force him somehow to tell her more of Atturn, of the Karn who had stood wearing Atturn's face and who had launched the fire bolt at them, who might have set upon them the monstrous creatures who had pulled them down. There was too much she did not know, could not know when the mind-seek refused to serve her.

Shortly after dawn, having eaten meagerly again of the dry stuff and been allowed to drink, they were marched on steadily across the plains. Stans walked well ahead of her. He seemed unsteady on his feet and now and then the Yurth beside him put out a hand to aid him with the impersonal manner of a machine doing some set duty.

They halted at intervals to rest, and were offered water at each such halt. The dry grass grew long here, sweeping to their knees and Elossa could trace no path in it. Still the party certainly moved as if they some well known trail and did not have to fear getting lost.

There was something about the horizon ahead, a kind of haziness she could not account for. But shortly before noon, or so she judged it to be by the sun, they reached the explanation for that. The plain ended almost abruptly in a cliff. It would seem that this level country was really a large plateau and to proceed they must descend to a country lying below, a far different country.

Whereas the plain forecast the swift coming of winter, the growth they now looked down on was lush, thick with leaves as it might be at the height of a good growing summer. Trees stood so close together that all one could really see for the most part was their tops, the leaves ruffled by gentle winds.

The leading guard went to the left a little and stepped onto the beginning of a stairway which had been cut back into the stone of the cliff. They followed single file, going down into that waiting lower land.

17

The luxuriant growth of vegetation in this lower land was beyond anything Elossa had ever known. Those valleys and plains in the east which the Raski cultivated to the best of their ability would seem desert borders compared to this. As the stair down the cliff side gave way to a road wide enough for six such guards as surrounded them now to walk abreast Elossa continued to wonder at the difference in this country.

Overhead trees arched, completely, she guessed, cloaking the road under their canopy. While the trees themselves were of new species. Between their trunks and lower branches climbed and looped thick vines which branched into stems so heavy with a bright purple fruit that they drooped downward near to breaking.

Around the fruit flew and climbed countless feasters—some feathered, some furred. Their squawks and cries led to a continual rise of sound. Yet none of the guard marching below glanced upward or seemed to notice any part of what lay on either hand.

There was a dank lushness to the very air of this woodland, scents both rank and fragrant hung as heavy as the fruit, clogged the nostrils and made the breath come faster as if one labored to catch lungfuls of the keener and more sterile air of the heights.

The road underfoot was well laid and Elossa noted that, for some reason, none of the thick undergrowth so much as hung out above it. Those blocks might in themselves generate some warn-off quality which kept the forest from intruding on the work of the builders who so challenged nature.

The way did not run straight. There were some trees of such a girth that it appeared their rooting could not be disturbed, so the road curled east or west about their bulk. When this was so and one glanced back it seemed that the road itself had disappeared from sight beyond each such curve.

Beads of sweat gathered along the edge of Elossa's hair, trickled down her face. This heat reached out to wrap her around until it seemed that every place her clothing touched her body the coarse fabric fretted and chafed her skin. Still the Yurth guard, having set on this path, did not pause or in any way abate their pace.

But all roads in time have an end and this one came as they rounded an isle of earth which gave root space to three giant trees, so smothered in vines and towering ferns that the whole looked as solid as a rock wall.

The crook in the road ended in an open space, also paved with the firmly laid stone blocks. Set flat in the surface of the center was an opening, square and without doors. Now they came to more stairs but this time the descent ran into depths below the surface of the ground.

It was darker as they went; still there was enough light to see about them. The stair curled around, leading ever down but following the walls of this well-like space in a spiral pattern. The lower they went the more the lush rich air of the forest thinned, though there was a current which Elossa could feel and it was fresh.

She tried to count the steps, hoping so to gain some idea of how deep this burrow went. But it was easy to lose count. And she disliked the atmosphere of the place more and more. Yurth life was mainly led in the open, under the sky, and with fresh winds about one.

They reached the end of that descent to face a passage running straight from the foot of the stairs. Along it at intervals torches set in rings fastened to the walls smoked and flared, the acrid scent of their burning strong.

That hall ended in another arch and Elossa near missed a step. Once again they fronted the same—or twin—stone face of Atturn, its open mouth stretched wide awaiting them.

Two of the Yurth dropped to hands and knees and crawled through. Then pressure on Elossa's shoulders forced her down into the same humble position, indicating that she must follow suit. Angrily she obeyed, shrinking as far as she could from any contact with the walls of that mouth opening.

There was a wide chamber beyond, walled as well

as floored with stone. As she scrambled to her feet she saw that there was a dais at the other end of the room and on it a seat high of back, wide of arm. Yet as large as that throne was it in no way dwarfed or belittled the man seated on it.

Red and black, crest of roached hair held high, this was he who had fronted them before the attack of the misshapen creatures. He was smiling as Elossa's guards dragged her forward, watching her as a sargon, had it more than rudimentary intelligence, might watch helpless prey advance within paw-crushing distance.

The girl held her head high, something in her responded with instant defiance to that smile, to the arrogant confidence the lord exuded, though to meet him stare for measuring stare was all she might do now.

The Yurth who had brought her there were as blank faced as ever. They were—maybe they were only now extensions of this Karn's will, his things, in truth swallowed up by Atturn.

"Lord." It was Stans who broke that silence. He elbowed past Elossa as if she were invisible, taking a stand immediately below the single tall step of the dais. "Lord King. . . ."

The dark eyes of the man broke contact with Elossa, turned to the Raski, so like him in body. That smile did not fade.

"You make common cause with Yurth. . . ." In Karn's voice that last word took on the sound of some degraded and degrading obscenity.

"I am Stans of the House of Philbur." The Raski had not knelt, save for the address of courtesy, he stood as one addressing an equal. "The House of

Philbur—'' he repeated as if those four words were in some manner a talisman which would admit him to the dominate company of Karn. "Is it thus that the Lord of Kal-Hath-Tan speaks with his kin?" He jerked his shoulders as if to point home that he went bound as a prisoner.

"You company with Yurth filth."

"I bring you Yurth for you to do as you will. Your servants took no time to ask."

So! Her vague distrust of Raski, in spite of all their seeming need of one another had been right! Lies— lies ran behind him to the very moments on board the wrecked ship when he had apparently agreed that they had common cause in questioning all tradition had built in the past of their two peoples.

Karn's probing stare was sharp. Elossa felt another probe—not Yurth contact clean and clear, no. This was a furtive nibbling at the outer defense of her mind, a desire to violate her inner being without the power to force the rape.

"Interesting," Karn remarked. "And how knew you of the Kal-Hath-Tan which is, Raski?"

"It was—is—that laid upon the House of Philbur, that we take blood price for Kal-Hath-Tan. In each age we take it."

"There is a blood price for Kal-Hath-Tan of a different sort, Raski." Karn made a slight gesture to indicate the two vacant-eyed Yurth before him. "Yurth filth here is slave. More bitter is this than death—is that not so, Yurth?" Now he spoke directly to Elossa.

She made no answer. Still Karn—or some alien power in this place—was seeking a way past her mind shield. She found such fumbling feeble so far, but that did not necessarily mean that it could not build in force, perhaps without warning.

Karn's lips, so like those of Atturn's mouth, moved in what might be silent laughter. His gaze on her was worse than any blow which he might have dealt physically.

"Yurth breaks—yes, Yurth breaks. And I find it good that this, your gift to me, kinsman, is female. Breeding of our humble slaves is slow—we lack many females. Yes, I find your gift good." He raised his hand again and the Yurth to Stans' right took a step backward and freed the Raski's hands with a quick slash of his bonds. "You claim House Blood of Philbur, kinsman. That also interests me. I thought that all our blood was gone."

"As for the Yurth—take it to the pens."

Elossa did not need the jerk on the cord about her wrists to bring her around. The hidden evil of this place was like a stinking mud rising about her feet, seeking to drag her down. She was willing enough to see the last of Karn and his "kinsman."

They left the audience chamber by a second door and traveled through such a maze of shorter and narrower passages that, though she tried to set each turn and twist in memory, she despaired of ever finding her way through them again.

At length she was shoved through a door into a room where there were more Yurth—women. None of them raised eyes to look at her as she half fell forward, being unable to help herself as her hands had not been freed. Instead those half dozen females of her own race stared blank-eyed before them. Two, she noted with horror, Karn's threat returning, had the big bellies of the pregnant. But they were all slack faced, as if empty of mind.

None of these wore the suits of the ship people; rather their robes could be the journey dress of the Pilgrims. But she recognized none of them as missing members of her clan. And she had no way of telling how long they might have been there.

Then the woman nearest her slowly turned her head. Her gaze fastened dully on Elossa's face and the horror of the mindlessness it suggested made the girl hurriedly edge away as the woman arose sluggishly to her feet and advanced toward her. To be touched by this—this *thing* wearing the guise of Yurth brought a scream very close to her lips.

But the woman passed behind her and a moment later Elossa felt a fumbling on the cords which bound her. Those fell away. Still blank of face the woman shuffled back to the pile of unsavory, stained couch pillows where she had first crouched and subsided again in the same position. Elossa, rubbing her wrists, moved back until her shoulders touched the wall and there dropped down to sit cross-legged.

Her gaze kept returning to the woman who had freed her. To look at this fellow prisoner suggested that the stranger was no different from her companions. Still, something had led her to come to Elossa's aid. Letting her head fall back against the support of the wall, Elossa closed her eyes.

That fretting at the edge of her mind-shield was gone. Very tentatively she released a small questing probe of her own. Nothing close to hand. If these here in this room and the other Yurth she had seen in the common dress were captured during the Pilgrimage then they had come here with powers equal to her own. Still those had seemingly been drained from them, leaving them empty and useless.

But the Raski had no such power. At least those of the outer world had not. They could be manipulated by Yurth hallucinations should just cause for such arise. What *was* Karn that he had been able to enslave those with gifts none of his race could claim?

"Karn is Atturn. . . ."

Only discipline of mind kept Elossa quiet. Who had sent that thought?

"You—where?" she shot out.

"Here. But be warned. Karn has his ways. . . ."

"How?"

"Atturn was a god. Karn is Atturn," came the not clear response. "He has ways of breaking minds— but not all. Some of us were warned in time . . . retreated. . . ."

Elossa opened her eyes slowly, looked to the woman who had freed her. This must be the one.

"Thank you. But what can we do?"

"I am not Danna." The correction came quickly. "She is broken. But still she can respond—a little. We work—we who still are true Yurth—to repair. But there are so few of us. No, do not look for me—we meet as mind speaking mind—we do not know each other otherwise lest in some ill chance the truth be riven from us. That death which came to Kal-Hath-Tan had strange, evil results. You have seen the twisted creatures who obey Karn in the first valley, those who trap all that wander into the inner lands.

"They are of the blood of Kal-Hath-Tan, but the

ruin of the fire which blasted forth tainted them.
They bear children from time to time as monstrous as
themselves. Karn was worked upon otherwise; he
was already learned in a strange way in secrets known
only to high priests and rulers. Of them a handful
were in a secret inner place when the end came to the
city. Karn became deathless, the incarnation so he
believes—so his people believe—of Atturn who was
never a deity of any grace or good. Karn has outlived
those who survived with him, always they sought
what is Yurth power—that of the mind. But they
sought it their own way—in order to deaden the spirit
of others. And much did they learn through the passing years. Now. . . ."

As if a door had been slammed between her and
the one who spoke there came instant silence. Elossa
closed her eyes but did not attempt mind-probe again.
The interruption had been warning enough.

Then speeding straight to her like a spear thrown
in anger came another mind-touch.

"Kin." It was not that word which was hearten-
ing, it was the very force with which it came to her.
Here was no evasion or warnings. Yet, dared she
respond? The small scraps of information she had
been fed suggested that Karn had resources to meet
Yurth power. Perhaps he could also, in some per-
verted way, ape Yurth call.

"Come in."

Fair invitation, or trap? Still she hesitated. How
deep had the rot reached in the Yurth who slaved for
Karn; could one of them serve him thus, too, helping
to betray some newcomer to actual takeover? Elossa
felt that she could not depend upon her own judg-

ment. With Stans she had been more than half convinced that he was willing to step free of the prejudices of his people, even as *she* had seen in that time of revelation in the ship the narrow folly—or what seemed so—of hers also. Yet Stans had indeed brought her here to Karn. Perhaps he had known from the very moment they left Kal-Hath-Tan where they were bound and why. He might have so betrayed others making the Pilgrimage before her.

"Come in," urged that other mind, laying open the door in a way which even Yurth seldom did and then only to those they trusted above all others. It was such an intimacy, such an invasion of the inner being that it only came at times of high peril—or honest shared emotion.

"Come in." For the third time, and now it did not ask, it demanded in some impatience, even anger.

Elossa drew upon the full sum of her energy. She might be making the worst mistake of her life, or she might be finding a defense against the worst Karn had spoken of with his vile suggestion. She shaped a mind-probe, only hoping that she would have the power to jerk loose in time, if again she had trusted wrongly. With that probe she did as the other ordered—she went in.

18

But she was so startled as that other touch met hers that she nearly broke contact by an instantaneous retreat, a blocking. For it was not a single mind which had demanded liaison with her. No, this was a combination of different personalities! And Elossa had never known this kind of union herself. The one acting-in-concert which her own clan had done was for building of some hallucination when extra strength was needed to hold such for a length of time. Even then, she, not having made the Pilgrimage, had never been one so called upon to lend her power to the general good.

Her momentary resistance vanished, she became a part of this union, and in her grew an exultation, a feeling of such confidence as made all her other small triumphs of the past seem as nothing at all.

"We are together!" It sounded as if those others, too, felt the same surge of near invincibility. "At last, kin, we are strong enough to move!"

"What would you do?" she asked that which she could not even yet sort into separate individual personalities.

"We act!" came the firm answer. "For long have we joined one to another, and yet another. We have hidden behind the slave covers Karn set upon us. For we needed more and more strength before we could go up against him. What he controls is alien to us; he has created such a barrier that we could not blast through. But now—now, kinswoman—with your strength added we await the final battle.

"Soon they will come for you that Karn may make you even as he thinks we are. Wait, go with them, but wait. When the moment comes—then we shall be ready!"

It was in Yurth blood to be cautious, ever wary, mistrusting to one's self for fear the power might seduce one to a downfall. All this distrust was aroused in Elossa as she listened. Yet she was impressed by the utter confidence of the multi-voice. And there was that in its argument which seemed logical. If Yurth, taken from the Pilgrimages—and perhaps elsewhere (she had no explanation yet for those wearing the ship's clothing)—had indeed pooled their strength, added force one to another, who knows what such an accumulation might accomplish. It would seem that this was indeed her best hope of escaping the fate she saw before her in this room of beaten women. She had a flash of speculation as to which of them were allied now in this composite voice.

"We must not act until Karn is about to use his own power," the voice continued. "We do not know if he can learn in any way from his own methods what we would do. Therefore, do not use mind-touch, kinswoman, until we come to you.''

The voice was gone. Elossa shivered at its vanishing. While it had been with her she had felt warm, at peace. Now that it had gone she could worry once more, foresee only too many ways in which failure lay. She closed her eyes again and drew upon her will, upon those techniques for conserving and strengthening inner power which she had been so carefully schooled to use.

But she was not given long so to arm herself, for the door opened and the grate of its opening aroused her, though it was not the Yurth she expected to see, those guards who would come to make her submit to Karn's unholy slave making. Rather it was Stans.

He slipped inside and closed the door behind him, standing then with his shoulders against it as if he would use his body to reinforce a barrier. None of the other women looked up, their faces remained blank. But he was staring straight at her, and she saw his lips move with exaggerated shaping as if he would send her some message which he must not say aloud. She tried to read as twice he went through that, and the third time. . . .

"Come in."

The same message as that other. But was he Karn's instrument? If she obeyed the Raski's order would it mean enslavement? This was not what the multi-mind had warned her of, but that did not mean that this was not as great a peril as what her kin had here faced and lost to.

That a Raski should summon mind-touch was so against all the customs of his race that she could not believe in this. But for the fourth time he was shaping the words, and his expression was one of strain. He had turned his head a fraction so one ear rested against the door as if he must listen for some danger without.

It was trust he demanded. Elossa weighed her present feeling for Raski against the facts of their journey together. They had saved each other's lives, yes. How much did that count against his words to Karn? Her inbred caution warred with another emotion she was not prepared to understand which she wished to press out of her mind altogether but could not.

At last she did as he wished. She sent a mental probe. Just as she had reeled and tried to withdraw from the multi-mind's meeting so did she know instantly that strange revulsion moved in him at her invasion. Yet as quickly he steadied himself, even as a man facing impossible odds for some point of honor which was even greater to him than life. She could read. . . .

And. . . .

Her strange instinct was right. What he had said to Karn—that had been a weapon of sorts, all he could seize upon at that moment. She read and learned.

Karn the impossible, the man who in the destruction of his city ages ago had, as she had earlier been told, continued to live, because he had already been deep in strange practices of the mind, disciplines of the body learned by chance by an obscure priesthood. They had wrought such changes, not by their own inner striving, but by the use of drugs and strange practices of control which could force hallucinations until the unreal became permanently real.

Fleeing the destruction of Kal-Hath-Tan a handful of priests, and Karn, had reached this other sanctuary—one they knew of old—to which even then they had retired at intervals with victims for their researching into unhealthy paths. Karn had lived, or was it a hallucination of life? At any rate here he ruled.

The Yurth from the ship—some had been captured, brought here, subjected to Karn's processes of domination. They too, lived. But they were indeed the hollow shells of what they had been. For they had not been subjected to that change which Yurth brought upon themselves when they assumed the burden of what they considered their irreparable sin.

When the new generations made the Pilgrimage some had been drawn into Karn's net by the same method he had used with Elossa, the call for help uttered in Yurth mind-touch. Thus the hidden master of the over-mountain land had built up his forces.

He had had no failures—outwardly. So he became in his own eyes, undying, all powerful, Atturn himself, that entity which had been the core of the research. One by one the priests had died, or Karn had brought death to them. But Karn remained ever in power. Now, now he had thought to gather his forces, to extend his rulership. He had been questioning Stans, striving to learn what lay open to his taking in the plains lands to the east.

"He read your mind?" Elossa demanded. For if Stans had lain as open to Karn as he was now to her then what hope had either of them for rebellion?

"He could not," Stans returned. "He was angry, and—I hope—troubled. But I am not one with him in Atturn. However, the fact that we are kin may not keep him from striving to break me. He has all which worked for him long ago—the drugs—the other things. But that takes time. He had not had me long enough in his hands."

Elossa made her decision. "Do even as you have done—play his liege man."

"But he will take you soon. You will become as these." Stans made a slight gesture to indicate the women about her, none of whom had seemed even yet to note his presence.

She might trust him from what she had read in his open mind, but it would be better not to provide him with any other information, unless she could hint that within herself lay some defense she had not yet tried.

"It may be that I can stand to him. If he holds in thrall all these Yurth then that must be exhausting to whatever power he summons. I am fresh come— and. . . ."

Stans stiffened. He turned to face her fully, his hands now balled into fists.

"They are coming!"

"They must not find you here." She was quick to recognize the additional peril in that. "Behind there." She pointed to one of the low couches on which the women sat. There was a small space between it and the wall—a very poor hiding place. But if they took her quickly—and she distracted their attention—it might serve.

He shook his head but she crossed swiftly and seized upon his sleeve.

"If Karn's men find you here then what good will you do either of us?" she demanded fiercely. "Hide, and later do what you can. Be Karn's man, perhaps he will bring you to see how he can enslave me. Then we can well have a chance there to act together.''

Stans did not look convinced, but he did push toward the divan. The unmoving women still did not lift their eyes as he flattened himself into hiding there as best he could. Elossa, chin up, summoning her best appearance of confidence, stood not too far from the door as if she had been pacing up and down as might a new taken prisoner.

It was not the Yurth who came for her, rather two towering, shambling creatures, distorted, demonic-headed Raski, plainly of the same breed as those who had first captured them, the tainted city stock.

They had to stoop to enter for their heavily mus-cled bodies were those of giants among their kind. And they slobbered from half-open mouths. Their near naked bodies gave off the stench of unwashed, even diseased flesh as they closed in upon her, each gripping an arm and dragging her toward the door. Nor did they glance around. Stans, she thought, was safe.

Once again she passed, firmly held by her two monster guards, through a number of passages, until they came into a room near as large as the presence chamber in which Karn had first greeted them. Here his throne was to one side, less impressive. The middle of the room was occupied by a huge represen-tation of Atturn. From the open mouth of that puffed, irregularly, trails of smoke, thin trails which did not rise to the ceiling, but rather wreathed around the mask-face as if it willed their clinging touch.

Elossa smelled the strange odors of the place. Was

the smoke one of the mind-bending drugs Stans had mentioned? If so there was no way for her to escape at least some of Karn's infective devices.

The master of this maze had directly before him a brazier of gleaming metal, along the edge of which played those lines of light as had been on the walls of the corridor behind the first of the Mouths. In ths, also, burned something which gave off smoke, and he leaned forward, was inhaling that, like a man gulping down some life-renewing fluid, his mouth open.

And. . . .

His face was changing. She watched, sure that she was viewing some hallucination achieved by the methods of the Raski priests. His countenance when she had entered had not been that of Atturn. Now, under her gaze the flesh stretched, altered, he was becoming Atturn once again, claiming the outward seeming of his god.

His eyes closed, he straightened up. The smoke` from his brazier had died away. Whatever burned there might be utterly consumed. But his mouth hung open in Atturn's malicious grin. Even the tip of his tongue protruded over his lower lip until he was the exact copy of the huge face before which her guards had stationed her.

Now, without opening his eyes, Karn spoke—his words strange to her, rising and falling with the steady beat of an invocation. Words and rhythm were a part of building hallucination as she well knew. Her own defense against this instantly clicked into action. She refused to look—either at the man or the face before her. Her eyes closed, she held them so with all the firmness of her will. Still the desire to open them, to see the face, gripped her.

It was moving—she *knew* it! The lolling tongue within the mouth was reaching out to grip her as had the mist tongue near taken Stans in the mountain corridor. No! That was not true—it was only what Karn tried to insert into her mind. Stans—she thought of the Raski—built his face up as a picture to fit over that of Atturn. Stans who had allowed her to read his thoughts in spite of all the horror his kind felt for such an act—Stans. . . .

To her vast astonishment that face she held in her mind became alive, not just a representation she used as a part shield against Karn's devilment. The lips moved, and in her thoughts a small and weak sound— wholly alien to Yurth touch—spoke:

"I . . . come. . . ."

Karn's trickery? No, she felt that had the master of this den managed to slip past her barrier his message would have been far more compelling. But Raski did not have the talent that was Yurth's, and perhaps, combined with drugs and hallucinations, Karn's. Then how had Stans reached her?

She felt the beat of the words Karn mouthed, and now she crooked her fingers, altered the rhythm of her breathing, did all she could not to fall into the insidious trap that offered to make her own body betray her.

There was a sudden check in the rhythm—Elossa opened her eyes. Stans was indeed there, within touching distance of Karn. The man who wore Atturn's face had not looked at him, but the face itself changed again. From assured maliciousness it began to register growing rage. The eyes snapped open.

Stans swayed as if those eyes were weapons, had flashed out at him some shattering force. And at the same time:

"Now!" So loud was that voice in her brain that Elossa, in turn, wavered, took a step or two toward the face in order to catch her balance again. But she was no longer aware of her body at all—all that did matter was the huge face confronting her, still wreathed in those tenuous trails of sickly smelling smoke.

Her will, all the talent which lay within her, joined with those others at the summons. She was no longer a person, a living being; instead her body became only a holding place in which the power being fed to her grew and grew. She wanted to scream, to fight back—to force out of her this monstrous thing which was crushing her. But instead she was a part of it, she could not deny it entrance.

It seemed that in her torment she would burst apart, that nothing formed of human flesh and blood could contain what gathered, strengthened, made ready. Without her knowing it her mouth opened in a soundless scream of torture. She could hold no longer. But it had gathered, become full grown to the greatest force it might ever obtain—and now—it struck!

19

It seemed to Elossa that she actually saw that spear point of pure energy speed outward from her. Did indeed that light become real to her eyes, or did she see it only by the Yurth sense?

Straight for Karn that was hurled. His hands moved so swiftly that she hardly saw the gesture until they were in place, palm outwards, shielding from her his Atturn face. Now she swayed where she stood, for her body shook and quivered as the force of the Yurth gathered in her, solidified there, then sped out.

There was no Karn, no Atturn there now.

What curled in the place of the man were flames, both black and red. Outward flared those flames. The heat from them crisped her hair, was searing torment to her flesh. Flames swallowed up the spear of force, strove to destroy it utterly.

Still she did not cook away to nothingness. But her consciousness retreated further and further. Elossa was near gone, what trembled and wavered here was only a vessel to collect and then dispense energy.

The flames of Karn were fierce flags whipping about her. From behind those there beat steady sounds, each of which struck her like a blow.

And. . . .

That which gathered in her, melded to speed forth, it was weakening, the flow was no longer steady, while the roasting heat of the Karn fire was something she had no strength to hold at bay.

On the very edge of her vision there was movement. Elossa could not turn her head to see what chanced there—she must hold steady—if she could hold.

"Ahhhhhhhhh—"

Sound slashed as might a wood axe brought against a young tree. The sounds which had beat upon her. . . . Elossa steadied, somehow made a plea, and gave herself a last fraction more freely. The power arose in her—for the last time she knew.

She held it, held it as long as she could, until she knew that her battered mind could contain it no longer. Then, as might a warrior in battle release a shout of utter defiance—tinged with despair—she loosed that final upflowing of Yurth talent—hurled it outward. . . .

The flames flared out and up. But this time she could see the spear of light out through them, break upon hands, hands which appeared in the heart of the flames.

"Ahhhhhh—"

Was that shriek of mingled pain and fear real, or part of a hallucination? Elossa wavered to her knees.

She was empty! The power went out of her so suddenly that it was as if the very bones which supported her flesh had been withdrawn, leaving her no firmness of body at all. She braced herself with her hands upon the floor, her arms as tautly straight as she could hold them.

The flames died, were utterly gone. She had failed! Karn stood there still erect, invincible. Behind him in a half crouch was Stans. The Raski's face was set in a grimace, his lips were pulled a little away from his teeth, he looked at that moment as one rendered near as monstrous through torture as the misshapen creatures they had been captured by in the valley.

His breath came in great gasps, as if he could not draw enough air into his lungs. But now he launched himself at Karn, his hands out, his fingers crooked as if they were claws to tear the undying king into bloody shreds.

He moved jerkily as if he were in some manner crippled, yet was so will bound to what he would do that he could make even a maimed body obey this last small attack.

His strength came against Karn. The king had taken no notice of his kinsman, but had stood statue still in the same position in which Elossa had last seen him, erect, his hands before his face.

Now those hands dropped, not as if he had lowered them, but as if there were no longer any strength left in the muscles which held them so. The flesh covering them appeared pallid, shriveled.

As his arms hung limp at his sides Karn took a step forward, then stumbled, fell to his knees on the floor beneath the one-step dais which had held his second throne. He was within touching distance of Elossa now.

But, seeing his face, she cringed away. Though his eyes were open, set, only white showed between the lids. There was a terrible, sickening change in his face, a writhing between Atturn and Karn, as if a last struggle between two personalities were in progress within him.

He began to crawl and Elossa pulled her body out of his path, edging around herself to watch him. Though he seemed blind, yet he was led toward the screen, the mouth of Atturn.

"No!" Stans sprawled down after the king. "He must not enter!"

As the king, he crawled, seemingly with little strength left. His strained face was also turned to the waiting Mouth.

"He must not . . . go . . . to . . . Atturn!" he gasped.

Elossa strove to draw upon any remnants of energy still in her. She opened her mind, sent out a plea for that which had been hers. But there came no answer. Had the multi-voice been riven forever?

Stans crawled on, and so did Karn blindly advance. Then the Raski launched himself once more in attack, sending his body before the path of the king as a barrier. When Karn reached him Stans grappled, holding the king by main force against struggles which, Elossa saw, Karn aimed not at his captor but rather to free himself.

His blind-eyed face was ever toward the stone image, his neck strained until his head was at a strange stiff angle. But Stans kept his grip on the struggling body of the king. As much as the Raski tried to hinder him, still Karn pulled forward, winning the length of a finger, the width of a palm, with dogged push.

Stans raised a fist, drove it full force into Karn's face. Elossa heard the dull sound of that blow, saw the involuntary rock of the head when it landed. Yet the blankness of expression did not change, the eyes remained rolled up and blind.

"No!" Stans' voice shrilled. "Not . . . to . . . the Mouth!"

His frenzy of struggle was enough to bring Elossa crawling toward them also. There must be a reason for Stans' need to keep Karn from the representation of the "god"—if god the Mouth was. She reached forth a hand and caught at Karn's arm, digging her fingers into the black and red fabric which covered it. But what she so held might well be made of metal, so unyielding was the substance of his tense flesh.

However, her effort, small though it was, when added to Stans', seemed enough to halt the crawl for an instant. Then, in their hold, Karn appeared to go mad. His struggles were the writhing of something totally divorced from reason. He flung his head around and down, snapping at Elossa's hand with his teeth. The pain of that wound loosened her hold and he jerked free.

With one great final effort he flung himself forward, beating Stans flat against the flooring with that lunge. One arm was thrown up and out. His hand curved around the edge of the lolling tongue. The girl saw the strength of the pull he exerted to use that to draw himself on and up into the Mouth.

Stans got up to his knees. He joined his hands together into a single fist. Raising that above his head he brought it down in a hammer blow on the nape of Karn's neck, even as the king had caught at the tongue with his other hand and was well on his way to drawing forward into the Mouth.

Karn fell, his forehead hitting the tongue. There was a sound then which cut through Stans' panting, a sound which seemed to Elossa to echo sickeningly through the whole room. The body, which a moment before had been taut, tense with effort, relaxed, slipped down, though the one hand still lay, fingers laced about the edge of the tongue.

Stans lurched away. There was a dull horror in his eyes.

"He . . . if he had gone through . . ." he said in a shaking voice. "He could have lived and lived and . . . lived. . . ." His voice scaled upward and his body was shaking so that he could not control his hands but held them out in front of him now, quivering, staring at them as if he had never seen them part of him before.

There was another sound in that chamber, though it did not cancel out that of the blow which still echoed to Elossa. She looked up at the face and then cried out. Enough strength returned to her to clutch at Stans, dragging him back and away from the Mouth.

For the representation of Atturn was crumbling, falling in great jagged pieces of stone. These thudded down on the head and shoulders of Karn, hiding near half of his body.

Elossa pressed the back of her hand tightly across her mouth to stifle a scream. For behind that screen, as she thought the Face and Mouth had formed, there was. . . .

Nothing! Rather a curtain of darkness which negated all normal light. It did not reach to either wall of the chamber, rather was like a section of utter black forming an inner structure of its own.

The Face and Mouth had gone. Now the darkness itself was rifting apart from side to side. Objects within they could see dimly, without knowing what such might be. But as the darkness tore and vanished, so did that which it had held. Now they could sight bare wall where they stood.

The shadow dwindled, seeped into the rock on which they crouched. Then all that remained was the half-buried body. Elossa could not turn her gaze from that. The defense of the Yurth had been torn from her.

Stans had crawled to her side. Now he pulled at her, thrusting his face close to hers.

"OUT!" He mouthed that order, jerking her toward the door through which she had been brought.

Somehow his order carried weight enough to get her started. But she retreated on her hands and knees, his hand impatiently urging her along whenever she grew faint.

Then they were out of the place of sickly scents, of death, and such illusions as she could no longer raise the strength to battle.

"Free. . . ."

No loud voice in her mind now, instead a whisper of near exhaustion.

Stans turned his head from where he had collapsed against the wall, only that support keeping him from sliding directly prone.

"Free. . . ." But he had said that aloud—and the other had been the multi-voice.

They were free indeed—but Yurth could not have done it without Raski. It had been Stans' actions back there in Karn's chamber to which much of the triumph belonged.

"Yurth," she said slowly, "and Raski. . . ."

He gave a sigh. "This. . . ." His glance went beyond her as if viewing all the length of the burrows underneath the earth. "Was evil of Raski—we did not stand guiltless after all. Raski and Yurth—perhaps something may now come of that thought we two shared in Kal-Hath-Tan after all."

She was so tired, so tired it was an effort to raise her hand from where it lay limp beside her knee. But this time she was the one to hold out palm and fingers in a gesture of union. Nor did she shrink, even in her mind, when his grasp closed about hers.

"Raski and Yurth—and freedom for both."

"True." The voice in her mind was stronger, a little eager, life was flowing back.

DAW

DAW

HEROIC FANTASY!

Do you long for the great novels of high adventure such as Edgar Rice Burroughs and Otis Adelbert Kline used to write? You will find them again in these DAW novels, filled with wonder stories of strange worlds and perilous heroics in the grand old way: